THE SECRET NOTEBOOK

D.A. D'Aurelio

CAPSTONE EDITIONS
a capstone imprint

The Secret Notebook is published by Capstone Editions,
an imprint of Capstone.

1710 Roe Crest Drive
North Mankato, Minnesota 56003
www.capstonepub.com

Library of Congress Cataloging-in-Publication Data is
available on the Library of Congress website.

ISBN: 978-1-68446-192-9 (hardcover)
ISBN: 978-1-68446-193-6 (ebook PDF)

Summary: Riley Green is certain her lie detector pen
will get her the status she craves in a school full
of kids from D.C.'s most powerful families. Her plan
collapses when her invention idea is stolen, her
favorite teacher goes missing, and a mysterious threat
shows up in the schools and offices of the D.C. elite.
Before Riley's teacher disappears, she entrusts Rile
with her most prized possession, the lost notebook of
Nikola Tesla. Now, Riley and her friends must protect
the notebook from thieves who want to steal it—and the
dangerous invention it holds. When Riley finds another
secret, she must decode the mysterious message before
it's too late. Her teacher's life depends on it.

Design Elements (old book pages) by Shutterstock/
Valentin Agapov

Cover art by Teresa Martinez

Designed by Tracy McCabe

Printed and bound in China.
3322

For my inventive husband, Mike

"I don't care that they stole my idea.
. . . I care that they don't have any
of their own."

—Nikola Tesla

1

TRUTH OR LIE DETECTOR

The train into D.C. smelled like perfume and coffee breath, but at least Mom and I had a seat. My presentation board bumped around on my lap. I held on tight, protecting it from getting damaged. Today, I was revealing my newfound talent to the class.

Ever since I could remember, I'd been trying out potential talents with disastrous results: dance (too tall and lanky); softball (strike zone too big); soccer (can't use my hands); magician (I don't want to talk about it); competitive kite flying (you definitely don't want to know!).

I agonized over what my thing could be. It had to be something cool, something unique, something I could own. Finally, my class took a field trip to the Spy Museum, and I was the only one who completed the simulated spy mission. That had to be it. I was obviously talented at spy stuff.

I especially liked the gadgets and technology for solving crimes, so for this year's Invention Convention, I had created a lie detector pen. The idea came to me when I found out that when someone writes down a lie, their handwriting changes. It was true. I did the research, and I was happy to say my pen could bust liars.

My right leg shook with nervous energy, which made no sense at all. Energy, by definition, is another word for power. I wasn't powering anything with my shaky leg, although I could probably start an engine with the amount of movement going on. I was trying to release energy, and somehow that seemed to help.

Mom quickly picked up on my nervous habit. "Don't worry, Riley, your invention is terrific," she said, expertly balancing her coffee while scrolling through the news on her phone. "I could use one of those lie detector pens around the office."

"Really? You think you might catch someone lying?"

"You never know." She wiggled her eyebrows.

Mom was an administrative assistant for a high-ranking senator, and she knew everything that went on in her office. Maybe my lie detector pen would help her to know even more.

"I wish I had a better prototype to show the class. All I have is this taped-up pen with a mood sensor on the outside."

"You'll do fine." She patted my leg.

The train stopped, and a gust of cold air blew in with new commuters. I pulled the skirt of my school uniform down to my shins, but it didn't help much. *Come on people, hurry up.* I wanted to have enough time to test my invention on my friend Henry before school. He was probably incapable of lying, but I wanted to know for sure. Plus, I'd thought of a great question to ask him.

The chimes of the Metro rail rang, and a recorded voice came over the loudspeaker. "Next stop, Union Station. Doors opening. Step back to allow passengers to exit."

Mom and I marched along with the crowd to the corner of Constitution and First, passing busloads of enthusiastic tourists ready for a long day of sightseeing.

Henry was waiting in our usual meeting spot in front of the Senate office building. He was staring at his cell phone and snapping his lucky orange wristband. He never took that thing off even though it was filthy and whatever inspirational message was on it had worn off years ago.

I gave Mom a quick hug before she headed off to work.

"Have a good day, kids. Only two more days until spring break!" she said.

Henry waved. "Bye, Ms. Green."

We took the same route every day: one block down First Street, past the Supreme Court building and Library of Congress, then straight to school.

"Let's stop for a minute. I want you to test my lie detector pen."

"Why?"

"Um . . . because I need another handwriting sample," I said, scratching my nose.

"You're not going to catch me in a lie. Besides, my handwriting is so sloppy you wouldn't be able to read it anyway."

He had a point, but it was worth a try. "Come on. I'll tell you what to write." I stopped at a nearby bench and handed Henry my lie detector pen and notebook. "First write, 'My name is Henry Marino, and I'm in sixth grade at Washington Prep Academy.'"

Henry huffed but wrote it anyway.

"Now write, 'My name is Maximus, and I think Riley is super-dumb and annoying.'" I *hoped* this was a lie.

"Ha!" he blurted out. "Really, Riley?"

"Just write it, please. It's for research." I crossed my fingers behind my back.

Henry wrote one line under the other, and I compared the two handwriting samples. Relief bubbled up inside and burst out in a smile. "Aha! You lied. You don't think I'm dumb and annoying, which means you think I'm smart—"

"—and annoying, but only sometimes," Henry said.

"That's not what your handwriting shows. See how the letters are taller in the second sentence, and the writing is darker? That's a sure indication of a lie. If this pen was the actual finished product, it would have a computer chip inside that could detect all the subtle details." I nodded, looking for him to agree with me, but he looked blank. "On top of that, the mood sensor on the outside turned from blue to brown, which means you were uncomfortable writing this."

Henry pushed his glasses up the rim of his nose and studied

the two handwriting samples. "That's cool," he said.

"Heck, yeah, it's cool!" I put the notebook back in my bag. "With any luck, I'll be chosen for the state Invention Convention, and someone from the FBI will be there and offer me a million dollars for my idea, or, even better, make me a junior agent."

"That would be amazing—but not likely," said Henry.

"It could happen." *Hey, I was allowed to dream.*

"Are you still keeping your invention a secret?" I peeked at the large black bag Henry held at his side.

"Yep, you'll have to wait for Dr. Schwartz's class. It's pretty awesome," Henry said.

"It doesn't explode, does it?"

"No, it's way better than that," he answered. "I just hate getting up in front of the class. I'm so bad at it. No matter how many times I practice, it never gets any easier."

"Really? I didn't think you were *that* shy," I said, surprised.

"I'm not shy around people I know. It's crowds," he said. "It's hard to explain."

"Well, I'll applaud for you," I promised.

Henry smiled. "Thanks."

We sprinted up the white marble steps of our school, the outside of which was surrounded by tall columns. Columns were a big thing in Washington, D.C. Most buildings had at least a few, probably because they looked strong and intimidating.

"I have to stop by the orchestra room," Henry said. "I'll meet you in class." He hurried off toward the music department.

"Okay, but I bet my invention is better than yours!" I called after him as I headed to first-period STEM class. The school still had that morning quiet before the storm of kids came rumbling in.

Down the hall, my favorite teacher unlocked her classroom door. Dr. Schwartz was easy to spot. She had one long streak of gray in a head full of black, curly hair, like she'd been bitten by a zombie skunk. I thought it made her look smart and sophisticated.

She liked to call me her apprentice and I didn't mind that at all. I wished I had STEM last period, so I could have something to look forward to all day.

I hurried to catch up. "Hi, Dr. Schwartz!"

"Good morning, Riley."

She flipped on the lights. We both froze. It looked as though a tornado had ripped through her classroom in the middle of the night. Papers were scattered across the floor, chairs toppled over, and every drawer and filing cabinet emptied. Dr. Schwartz covered her heart as if it might jump out of her chest. Her perfect classroom was a complete disaster.

"Who could have done this?" I asked in a whisper.

She shook her head slowly, as if it hurt to move. We stepped over books and debris. Dr. Schwartz stopped in the middle of the wreckage. I followed her stare to the whiteboard. Written in red marker were the words *CEASE AND DESIST OR DIE!*

2

INVENTION DECEPTION

Did that say *die*? I reread it, looking for a "just kidding" or "made you look" kind of comment, but there was nothing to indicate that it was a joke. The classroom was strangely still, like it was a single frame in a stop-motion video. A storm had roared through a short while ago, leaving wreckage behind.

Dr. Schwartz picked a few papers off the floor with a shaky hand.

"Why would someone destroy your classroom?" I asked.

"I don't know. For the past few days, I'd thought I was being followed, but I dismissed it as my imagination." She gazed around the room as if trying to make sense of it all.

I picked up Dr. Schwartz's chair, which had been thrown on its side. She placed her briefcase on the desk.

"What does 'cease and desist' mean, exactly?" I asked.

"It means stop immediately. They want me to stop my life's

work." She slumped down into her chair. "I was afraid this might happen one day."

Dr. Schwartz thought she might get a death threat? That wasn't usually an occupational hazard for a schoolteacher.

"I'll go get Dr. Chen." I dropped my backpack on the floor and leaned my presentation board against her desk.

"Wait, Riley! Don't tell anyone besides Dr. Chen. I need to trust you." She stared at me as if her life depended on it. *What if it did?!*

I sprinted toward the front office, taking long strides down the hall. The principal was a busy man and students usually needed an appointment to see him. *Should I interrupt or would I get in trouble? What was I thinking? This was an emergency!* I ran full tilt and barged right in.

"Dr. Schwartz's classroom was ransacked," I said with dramatic urgency.

The principal dropped his donut into his coffee mug. The black brew splashed onto his desk. "Goodness, Riley, you startled me."

"Someone destroyed Dr. Schwartz's room and left a death threat!"

"What?" His face tangled in disbelief.

"Please! You have to come right away!"

Dr. Chen scurried down the hall. His keys and loose change jingled all the way. When he saw the disaster, he froze. "What the . . . ?"

I was pretty sure he wanted to swear like a sailor, but instead, he held in the bad words like a mom would do.

"Don't touch anything," he said. "I have to notify the police."

"Can I take my presentation board and backpack?" I asked, remembering I'd left them here when I ran to his office.

"Yes," he said, distractedly. "But where's Dr. Schwartz?"

"I don't know. She was right here a second ago."

"Dr. Schwartz!" we called out, but there was no answer.

"Let's go to my office. I'll call her over the intercom." Dr. Chen locked the door behind us, securing the evidence inside.

By now, students filled the halls and stole glances at Dr. Chen and me marching past them, obviously on a mission. Once kids caught wind of this scandal, it would spread like the common cold. One sneeze and the whole school would know.

When we reached his office, I thought maybe he'd like to mull things over and come up with a plan to catch the culprit.

So, Riley, what are your theories about Dr. Schwartz's classroom? Was it thieves, hoodlums, pranksters? We could use your advice.

I stood, waiting for an invitation to sit down. Dr. Chen had a few types of seats depending on the purpose of the visit—the comfy teacher/parent chair, the leather interrogation chair, and the plastic, guilty-beyond-a-reasonable-doubt chair. But he didn't ask me to sit in any of them.

He clicked on the intercom. "Dr. Schwartz, please come to the front office."

"What can I do to help?" I asked, inching toward the comfy chair.

"Tell your classmates you'll be having STEM class with Mr. Tisdell in the media center."

"Got it." I turned toward the door.

"And Riley . . ." Dr. Chen stopped me. "Don't tell anyone about the incident until I have the authorities investigate."

"Yes, sir." I dashed out of the office. *Was he serious?* My head was exploding with scandalous information, and I couldn't tell anyone? Not even Henry?

I scribbled a note—"ALL CLASSES WILL BE HELD IN THE MEDIA CENTER." Then I used the extra tape from my invention project to stick it to Dr. Schwartz's door.

"Hi, Riley Green Giant," a voice said from behind me.

An involuntary groan came out of my mouth. I was in no mood for Dillon Walker III and his smug smile, full of wires and brackets. Usually, kids looked cute with braces, but Dillon looked like he was chewing on metal so he could spit out nails.

"Ha, because I'm tall. Like I haven't heard that one before."

Who cared if his father was a Texas senator and oil tycoon? *Most* kids at this school were the sons and daughters of high-ranking government officials.

"What's going on in there?" He jiggled the handle of Dr. Schwartz's locked door.

"Nothing. You can't go inside," I said.

"Why? Who put you in charge?"

I grinned. "Dr. Chen."

"Well, whatever happened, it wasn't me. I had nothing to do with it."

How did he know something happened? At that moment, I spotted a highly engineered pen in Dillon's hand, and the blood instantly left my face and dropped to my feet.

"What is that?" I pointed.

"Oh, this? It's a lie detector pen."

I couldn't breathe. I felt dizzy. It was as if Dillon had an invisible arm that shot out from his back and punched me in the gut. "Where did you get that idea?"

"It just popped into my head." He made a clicking noise with his tongue and opened his tri-fold board. His project was amazingly professional, like a display at the Spy Museum. His pen had a wireless connection with a light on the end that blinked red when it detected lies.

My entire dream of a career in criminal science was crumbling before my eyes. I slid my presentation board behind my back. I couldn't let him see my lie detector pen since it paled in comparison to his. "How . . . ? You couldn't have . . ."

"It's amazing how many ideas you can come up with when you know where to look, and how to listen." He smirked.

That was it. He had it coming. "You STOLE my idea!"

He blew out a laugh. "Riley, Riley. You need to work smarter, not harder." He tapped his finger on his horribly hollow head.

The blood rushed back into my face and I had an almost uncontrollable urge to throw my precious pen at him. If I hadn't been so bad at archery, I might've done it, impaling him through his cold, cold heart. But my aim was as bad as my patience.

I tried to think of the perfect comeback as he turned to leave.

Usually, I blurted out whatever was on my mind, sometimes too much. But around Dillon, I was like an emoji. I made all kinds of facial expressions but couldn't find the words. I knew I'd think of a stinging comeback later, but by then he would be long gone.

3

DETECTIVE RILEY GREEN, SUPER SLEUTH

There was no way Dillon and I just happened to come up with the same idea. Our minds did *not* think alike. He lied so easily and didn't show any of the telltale signs: feet shuffling, involuntary itching, avoiding eye contact, stuttering. It wasn't fair. Dillon could say whatever he wanted, and I would have to prove him wrong.

I grabbed my lie detector pen out of my backpack and held on tight. It turned burnt orange, matching my hostility. At least my invention had a mood sensor that told me when I was about to explode. I grabbed my presentation board and stomped down the hall.

"What's going on?" Henry asked, catching up to me.

"Dillon stole my idea. That's what's going on. He has the exact same invention!"

"No way! How did that happen?"

"I'll tell you how it happened. He obviously confiscated private information using sophisticated surveillance equipment or sent an undercover spy to infiltrate my research."

"Why do you talk like you swallowed a dictionary for detectives?"

I sighed, blowing out some tension. "My dad used to read old Raymond Chandler books. You wouldn't know him, but he wrote famous detective stories, starring Philip Marlowe, super sleuth. I guess I'm carrying on the tradition." Plus, I thought it made me sound confident and smart. I could have been wrong about that.

"Here's an idea. Why don't you use your lie detector pen on Dillon?" Henry raised an eyebrow.

That thought had crossed my mind, but Dillon was such a master at lying, it might not work on him. Plus, he would never go for it.

"What am I going to do, strap him to a chair and force him to write, 'Riley is the true inventor of the lie detector pen'?" That was the fatal flaw in my design, I realized, and I had no idea how to fix it. The suspect had to write down his or her side of the story. "Come on, we're having class in the media center."

"Why? What's wrong with Dr. Schwartz's room?"

Enough with the questions already. I wanted to tell someone about the criminal activity at school—perhaps even *needed* to tell someone. If I didn't, I might have some kind of internal combustion. I knew Dr. Schwartz trusted me, and I trusted

Henry. I pulled him around the corner. "I'll tell you, but you have to swear not to tell anyone." He nodded. That ought to cover me. I whispered the juicy details.

"Do they know who wrecked the classroom?"

"No, but there was a message written on the whiteboard." I paused for dramatic effect. "It said, 'Cease and desist or die.'" I made air quotes around the last part.

"Don't do that," Henry said.

"Do what?"

"The air quotes thing. Nobody does that anymore." He shook his head.

"Okay, fine. I was just telling you the exact words. It said *die*! Isn't that scary?"

Henry shrugged. "They probably have surveillance cameras so they can see who did it."

Of course, security cameras. They were practically foolproof lie detectors. "But the perpetrator could have been wearing a disguise or a hoodie. Whoever did it was strong enough to wreck the classroom and must have had the legal background to write 'cease and desist' instead of 'stop or else.' Only lawyers say stuff like that."

Henry lowered his head and raised his eyes. I knew that look and I knew what he was about to say, so I went ahead and said it for him. "Riley, you really need to stop spending so much time at the Spy Museum."

"That's right," Henry said. "The last time you got involved in suspicious activity, you ended up stuck in a closet for an entire class period because you thought our substitute teacher was a secret agent."

"He was an imposter, I tell you," I said with conviction. "He didn't know anything about the subject matter."

"He might've been a bad teacher, but he wasn't a spy," Henry said.

"Then how do you explain his strange accent?" I countered. "Sometimes he sounded German, and other times he sounded Jamaican. That's unnatural."

Henry didn't respond. He turned the corner and started toward the media center. He obviously didn't want to get wrapped up in any subterfuge, which is an awesome word I picked up at the Spy Museum. It means deceiving someone by misleading them, more or less.

"I just want to find out who did it," I said. "The person who destroyed Dr. Schwartz's room seemed to be looking for something, and wants Dr. Schwartz to stop her life's work." I made stupid air quotes around "life's work" and quickly pulled them back.

"It's probably just a prank that went too far. They'll find out who did it," Henry said.

Or, even better, I'd find out first.

"Maybe it was Dillon," I said. "If he's capable of hijacking my invention, he could vandalize a classroom."

The threatening-a-teacher part I wasn't so sure about.

Henry shook his head.

He was probably right. I should stay out of it. But if I could find out who'd threatened our teacher, maybe I could show off my criminal science talent, and people would believe I was the real inventor of the lie detector pen. Then I could still be known as Detective Riley Green, super sleuth.

4

TOUGH COMPETITION

The enthusiasm I'd had for the Invention Convention faded into absolute dread. My incredibly original idea now looked like an ordinary product if *Dillon Walker* could come up with the same invention.

Today, we were presenting our ideas in class, and in a couple weeks, we'd compete in the schoolwide Invention Convention. Only one invention—one *single* invention—would be chosen to represent our school at the state competition.

Students filed into the media center and searched for a seat. I studied my classmates—who were now also my competition. Some of the students looked ready and confident. Others looked nervous and fidgety, like me. I tied my hair back in a ponytail, took it out and tied it again, then tied it again, then . . .

"What are you doing?" asked Henry.

"Waiting for class to start." I let go of my hair but then my right leg went into turbocharge. I couldn't sit still.

Dillon sat in the back of the room testing his cheater project on a friend and laughing. His lie detector pen was so much better than mine. It was obvious he'd had help. His father had probably hired an engineer to build it. But once again, I didn't have proof.

The death grip I had on my pen made the mood sensor turn a muddy brown. *Perfect.* I dropped it on the table and blew on it to change the color back to blue.

Just when I thought things couldn't get any worse, Valerie sat down at our table. She was super-competitive and came from a long line of government officials. Her ancestors had more titles than the royal family. Right now, her father was speaker of the house, so Valerie thought she was speaker of everything else.

"Whatcha got there?" she asked.

"It's a pen that can tell when someone is lying," I told her. "I'm going to be a criminologist."

"What's a criminologist?"

"It's someone who uses science and technology to analyze evidence." I watched her expression for any sign of amazement. She looked mildly amused.

"Really? Does your pen actually work?"

"Yes, the pen collects data and sends it to a computer program. If there are any inconsistencies in the handwriting, the person is most likely telling a lie. But it's not hooked up right now," I said.

"Too bad. I wanted to ask you some questions to see if you were lying." She flipped her hair so that it lay perfectly over her right shoulder.

"What's that supposed to mean?"

She rolled her eyes. "No offense, Riley, but you need to use that pen on yourself."

I felt another punch in the gut. I wanted to shrink into a particle of dust and float away. Why would she even try to disguise her insult with, "No offense, Riley"? Whenever someone says that, you know they definitely plan to offend you.

"I'm not a liar, Valerie," I shot back.

I *wasn't* a liar—not anymore. That was a long time ago. I'd told a couple of lies because I was trying to fit in at this super-snooty school, and Valerie wouldn't let me forget it. I wished I'd never said my mother was a senior advisor to the president and my dad was on assignment with the CIA. Who knew everything that happened in this town was common knowledge? D.C. was obsessed with politics. You couldn't go two minutes without being reminded of the political news of the day. It was like living on an island and being reminded of the ocean. It was right in front of your face.

"Okay, Valerie. How about we both use my lie detector pen when I get it hooked up? You can ask me any question."

"No, thanks." She shrugged.

I grumbled on the inside but said "Fine" out loud. "What's *your* invention, anyway?" I asked.

She sat up straight and smiled like a game show model.

"It's shoes with an adjustable heel. You can make them low for day . . . " She pulled out the heel. "And higher for night."

"Clever, but are you sure that hasn't been invented already?" I could tell she hadn't thought to check that important detail.

Her fake smile turned into a frown. "I doubt it." She got up and walked away.

Good. I didn't want to talk to her anyway.

At this point, I was in full sulk mode and wanted to be done with my presentation.

Mr. Tisdell called up the first presenter. "Reagan Albright, please show us your invention."

Reagan jumped up and rolled her presentation to the front of the room. "My idea is called the Scootcase. It's a carry-on suitcase combined with a motorized scooter, so you can sit on your luggage and drive around the airport." She went on to explain the details.

How cool was that? My competition was tougher than I thought. I'd have to impress everyone with my knowledge of in-depth interrogation.

This all would have been easier if Dr. Schwartz were here. I didn't even get a chance to show her my lie detector pen. Why would someone want to hurt a STEM teacher anyway? Was she an eccentric genius who worked for the CIA, decoding classified information? Did she have an antidote for biological weapons?

"Riley Green, you're up next," announced Mr. Tisdell. *Wait. I wasn't ready! Go to a commercial!* I snapped out of my imaginary detective show and walked to the front of the class.

I took a deep breath, which was what my mom always told me to do when I was nervous, except my breathing was entirely too loud. *Thanks, Mom.* Mr. Tisdell gave me an encouraging smile, so I started right in.

"My invention is a lie detector pen. It can identify truthfulness based on handwriting samples." I held up the pen. "Studies have shown that when someone writes down a lie, their handwriting changes. An accelerometer inside the pen would detect the speed and movement of each stroke. Those readings would be transmitted into a simple program I coded to identify inconsistencies in the writing." *So far, so good.* My classmates seemed genuinely interested, and the butterflies in my stomach had settled down. "The outside is covered with a thermotropic liquid crystal that is the same technology used in mood rings. This crystal would reveal the stress level of the writer . . ."

The crackle of the intercom interrupted my riveting presentation.

"Mr. Tisdell, please send Riley Green to the principal's office!"

The butterflies in my stomach took flight again, as if they were being chased by a deranged bird.

"*Ooooh*, you're in trouble," taunted Dillon. I flashed him a squinty evil eye that shot ice-cold daggers. It seemed to have no effect on him, but I felt better anyway.

"She'll be right down," Mr. Tisdell replied to the principal. "Riley, you can finish your presentation later."

I hung my head. Had I done something wrong? Had I unintentionally offended someone? *Wait a minute.* I bet the principal wanted to ask me about this morning and my theories on the case of the ransacked classroom. I lifted my head. Let the investigation begin!

5

THE INTERROGATION

Down the hall, a few police officers converged on the front office, and for a split second, I thought Dad was one of them. That was impossible because he'd been gone four years now. But every time I saw a police uniform, my heart skipped a beat, like it had a spontaneous second of silence.

The police must've been called to investigate Dr. Schwartz's classroom. But the response seemed excessive for an ordinary prank. This must be serious. They smiled as I zoomed past and peeked into the principal's office.

"Come in, Riley," called Dr. Chen.

An officer built like an armored military vehicle sat in the plush teacher chair.

"This is Sergeant Jackson. He's investigating the criminal activity that occurred at school this morning." Dr. Chen motioned to the officer.

Sergeant Jackson turned in his chair to face me. Police equipment dangled from his uniform and he held a small laptop. "I met your dad a long time ago, Riley. He was a good man."

I let out my automated response, honed by years of having to talk about Dad even though it made me uncomfortable. "Thank you. That's kind of you to say. We miss him a lot."

Dr. Chen cleared his throat. "Riley, we want to know what Dr. Schwartz said to you this morning."

"Is she okay?" I asked.

"We don't know. She's not here and her car is gone, so we think she left on her own. But we want to make sure she's safe," said Dr. Chen.

"Do you think the threat is real?"

"We take every threat seriously," said Sergeant Jackson. "You were the only person to talk to her this morning, and we want to know exactly what she said."

I paused. Dr. Schwartz didn't want me to tell anyone besides the principal. Did that include the police? I guessed not.

"Right . . . well . . . Dr. Schwartz and I found her classroom vandalized at approximately seven-fifty this morning. At first, I considered the cause to be an inside job, possibly some teenage thugs. But the damage was very extensive for amateurs. When I saw the whiteboard defaced with a violent message . . ."

"Riley!" Dr. Chen interrupted. "Can you just tell us what Dr. Schwartz said?"

I guessed that meant they didn't want to hear my junior agent theories. "Okay, I specifically remember her saying she thought she was being followed," I said, wiping my forehead.

Dr. Chen and the sergeant looked at each other with great concern. The officer typed feverishly into his laptop.

"Did she say anything else?" he asked.

"Um, she didn't say much else, just that 'cease and desist' meant they wanted her to stop immediately." I waited for the officer to finish typing.

"Have you told anyone else about the incident?" His dark eyes looked down his nose at me.

"No. Only Dr. Chen," I scratched my arm and blinked rapidly. I had told Henry, but technically he wasn't just anyone, he was my best friend. I clasped my hands together so that I didn't fidget. Of course the police were probably trained to detect even the slightest hint of a lie. I hoped I didn't look as guilty as I felt.

"If you remember anything else, please give me a call." He handed me his card. "And don't worry, we'll find your teacher."

"Okay." I got up and took a step toward the door.

"Hold on, Riley." Dr. Chen stood up from his desk. "Since you're here, I need your help with something." He followed me into the reception area, where a girl was seated on the couch. She was wearing a big plaid bow in her hair that matched her school uniform perfectly.

"I'd like to introduce you to Charlotte Mae Harris. This is her first day at Washington Prep." She leaped out of her chair like she was dismounting a balance beam.

I stuck out my hand to shake. She stared at it for a couple

seconds and then shook it. Shaking hands was an absolute requirement in D.C. I was convinced most kids around here were taught handshaking before they could walk or talk.

"Charlotte Mae just moved to D.C. Her mother was appointed by the president to be secretary of agriculture, and we are honored to have Charlotte Mae here."

There was an awkward pause because this was usually the part when someone would say, "And Riley's mom is the ambassador to the United Nations," or some other fancy position like that. Mom wasn't a government official. She just worked for one.

"Oh, it's nothing. She's just my mama," Charlotte said in a deep southern accent that was foreign in these parts.

"Riley has been a student here since the second grade, and you two have the same schedule, so she'll be a terrific tour guide," Dr. Chen said.

"Thank you. That sounds fine," Charlotte Mae said.

Dr. Chen looked at his watch. "Okay, then. The bell is about to ring."

That was our signal to leave.

"Come on. We'll go find your locker," I said, starting down the hall.

"I'm so excited to be going to such a highly regarded school," she said.

"Yep, that's us, highly regarded," I said. More like high and mighty, but I should let her be the judge. "So, where did you move from?"

"I'm from Tifton, Georgia, home to the second largest magnolia tree in the nation, but it burned down a while back." She forced a laugh. "Tifton is a pretty small town, nothing like Washington, D.C."

"We just say D.C.," I told her.

"Excuse me?"

"We just say D.C. You don't have to say the Washington part," I explained.

"Oh . . . okay. Well, you can just call me Charlotte then, not Charlotte Mae."

"That works."

She sighed. "My mama got appointed to the president's Cabinet two weeks ago, and here we are. Can you believe it?"

"Well, you'll fit right in at this school," I said.

"Do you think so? That sure would be nice."

I sighed to myself. Getting a new student was great—I just wished we'd get one whose family wasn't a Washington insider, so I didn't feel like such an outsider.

6

MY SOUTHERN SIDEKICK

I sat in social studies trying to listen to Mrs. Morrison's lesson about the Age of Exploration, but my brain wanted to explore something else. All I could really think about was why Dr. Schwartz took off so fast. Where would she go in such a hurry? Then I remembered something else she'd said. Something I probably should've told the armored car police officer. She had said that they wanted her to "stop her life's work." Was that an important tidbit of information or was it okay to keep that between Dr. Schwartz and me?

If I were the kind of person who was interested in suspicious behavior (and I was), I would think Dr. Schwartz's actions were highly unusual. I trusted her, but something didn't feel right. Maybe I didn't know her as well as I thought.

The bell rang and the smell of today's lunch wafting around the halls triggered a loud growl in my stomach. I sniffed the air. "We're having Beef Wellington and potatoes au gratin for lunch today," I said after my super-sniffer had done its analysis. "The food here is pretty good."

"It smells wonderful. I'm so hungry I could eat anything, although my favorite food is pulled pork with Brunswick stew. There's nothin' like good barbecue to make you feel at home. Are there any barbecue places around here?"

"Um, I don't really know of any," I said.

Charlotte's smiled faded for the first time all morning.

"But don't worry. I'm sure there are barbecue places. I just don't know where they are."

She nodded. "Well, it's okay, my daddy makes a mean pulled pork sandwich. He's also a master at fried chicken and grit cakes. You should come over some time. Maybe he'll make us sausage and gravy. He makes it for my birthday every year. Am I talking too much? I talk a lot when I'm nervous. My mama says I exercise my jaw muscles like I'm training for an Olympic talking competition."

"No, it's fine," I said, grabbing my tray and heading straight to my regular table by Henry. I could use his help keeping up the chitchat with my new southern sidekick.

I placed my tray on the table. "This is Charlotte Harris. It's her first day here."

Henry stood up, wiped his mouth with his shirt sleeve, and shook Charlotte's hand. "Hi."

That was not the most quality introduction. In a school full of future politicians and general overachievers, Henry looked out of place, but in an adorable way. His shirt was usually untucked, his tie was often crooked, and his hair poked up like it wanted to jump off his head. At least he shook hands.

"So, how come you had to go to the principal's office?" Henry asked me.

"Dr. Chen wanted to talk to me about this morning," I said, like it was no big deal.

"What happened this morning?" Charlotte asked.

"Oh, um, our teacher tripped and fell in her classroom. She went home." I eyed Henry with tight lips. He got the hint.

"Is she okay?" Charlotte asked.

"As far as I know." I didn't want one more inkling of non-truth coming out of my mouth, or I would give it all away. I changed the subject. "So, what happened in STEM after I left?"

"I presented my invention," Henry said.

"Sorry I wasn't there to applaud. How did it go?" I asked.

"I got through it." He shrugged. "Everyone seemed to like it."

"What's your invention?" Charlotte asked.

"Yes, what *is* your invention?" I said.

"It's a gumball smasher blaster." Henry smiled a toothy grin, like he was rehearsing for a home shopping channel.

"I'm sorry. What did you say?" I asked, even though I'd heard every word.

"You know how gumballs are really hard to chew and could be a choking hazard?" Henry's face turned serious, as if he were solving a major international health crisis. "Well, not anymore.

First, you put your gumball in my smasher to make it easier to bite. Then, when you're done chewing your gum, you stick it in the special tube and new flavoring gets injected. When you want your gum back, you press a button, and it blasts out." Henry motioned as if the gum would shoot out like a rocket. "That last part is just for fun."

"That is revolutionary, Henry. How on earth have we survived without it?" I said slowly and deliberately. Actually, it sounded pretty fun, and I would probably want to buy one.

Henry tilted his head toward Charlotte. "If you haven't figured it out by now, that's Riley's sarcasm. She thinks she's being funny."

"I think she's hilarious." Charlotte laughed.

"Wait until I win first place," Henry said, his mouth full of potatoes.

"Did Dillon present his cheater project?"

Henry shook his head. "We ran out of time."

"What's a cheater project?" asked Charlotte.

"Dillon stole Riley's invention idea," Henry said.

"Why, that sneaky son of a snake. Can't you do anything about it?"

Charlotte had jumped on my team quickly. I was glad to have another ally. "I don't know how I can prove it. Dillon has been getting away with that kind of stuff his whole life."

"I'll be sure to stay away from him," Charlotte said.

Henry held up his fork. "Oh, I just remembered. We have to pick an inventor for a project we're doing after spring break.

Someone like Benjamin Franklin, Nikola Tesla, Steve Jobs. We have to do a research paper about him."

"About him?" I shot back. "There are plenty of female inventors too, you know, like Hedy Lamarr, who—"

Charlotte jumped in. "Invented a secret communications system during World War II!"

I didn't know whether to be impressed or annoyed. Spy stuff was my thing. "Yeah, well, there's a display about her at the Spy Museum. Have you ever been there?"

"No, I haven't done much sightseeing yet. My little brother would whine the entire time, so any place with the word *museum* in it is not on my family's schedule," she said.

"Riley has a season pass. She drags me there a lot after school," Henry complained.

"It's only fair I get to go to the Spy Museum because you're always dragging me to the American History Museum." I pointed my thumb at Henry. "He's a total history buff."

"Well, I'd like to go to both places. Maybe we can go to the Spy Museum tomorrow." Charlotte's face lit up. "That would be so much fun. You can show me around and teach me all about spying. What do you think?"

How could I say no to that much enthusiasm about the Spy Museum?

"Okay. Sure."

Tomorrow afternoon was the start of spring break, and sadly, I had no other plans.

7

A BOOK IN DISGUISE

Charlotte was my Velcro friend for the rest of the day. I wasn't sure if she stuck by me because I was considered her tour guide or if she actually enjoyed my company. Either way, I liked having a Velcro friend and thanks to a Swiss electrical engineer named George de Mestral, I liked Velcro too. Apparently, he got the idea when he went for a walk in the woods and he and his dog came back covered with burrs. He realized the seed burrs had little hooks on the ends that stuck to the fabric of his pants and his dog's fur. Now everybody uses Velcro.

The final bell rang, and we trotted down the front steps of the school.

"How do you get home?" I asked Charlotte.

"My daddy picks me up. How about you?"

"Henry and I walk to our parents' office together. My mom works for Henry's dad. He's a senator. It's only about a twenty-minute walk," I explained to my Velcro buddy.

"Cool. Will we be walking to the Spy Museum tomorrow?"

"Yep, it's not too far."

"Okay, there's my daddy." She pointed to a man standing next to an SUV waving like there was a prize for champion greeter. "Thanks for showing me around today, Riley. You're a really great tour guide."

"You're welcome. See you tomorrow." I waved goodbye.

I had to admit that meeting Charlotte saved the day from being a complete disaster. She was really nice for the daughter of a super-important government official. I half expected her to get sucked into the vortex of those well-connected kids who attempted to steal her attention. Even Dillon introduced himself like a true politician. His phony smile and firm handshake almost made me lose my lunch.

I strolled over to Henry in an informational fog. The bizarre events of the day spun around in my head. Since I'd already blabbed all the details to him, I could blab some more without worrying about keeping secrets. I couldn't wait to get started.

"I'm telling you, Henry, someone is out to get Dr. Schwartz."

"Are you sure you're not making things up?" he asked in his usual rational tone.

"Some perpetrator is passing out death threats, and you think it's my imagination?!"

"Well, maybe the *perpetrator* found whatever they were looking for in the classroom, and they'll leave her alone," Henry said.

We turned the corner onto First Street. "Maybe they wanted her briefcase," I said.

"That old briefcase? No way. Besides, she never goes anywhere without it."

"Exactly. Maybe she's hiding something in there." I wasn't going to let this go.

Henry shrugged. "I think the school and the police have this covered, Riley. There's not much we can do about it."

"You didn't see Dr. Schwartz. She looked so scared. Whoever destroyed her classroom wants her to stop her life's work. Maybe she has a recording of a top-secret conversation or she discovered a new planet inhabited by aliens." I whispered that last part because we were walking past the Capitol Building, and you never knew who might be listening.

"You should write this stuff down. Maybe you can make a movie someday."

"Good idea. Maybe I will."

I continued to come up with possible explanations until we arrived at the security checkpoint in the Senate office building. Henry and I put our backpacks on the conveyor belt and then walked through the metal detector. My favorite security guard, Oscar, was there to greet us.

"Well, hey there, Miss Green and Mr. Marino. Enjoying this glorious day?"

"Yes, sir. How about you?"

"I can't complain," he answered. We had the same conversation every day even if it was pouring rain.

Henry and I climbed the steps to the second floor and walked down the long hall where the New York State flag hung outside a door. We entered Senator Marino's office, which was bustling with the usual activity—keyboards clicking, phones ringing, people chatting. I stopped by Mom's desk and waved. She acknowledged my presence with a smile and continued her phone conversation.

We did the same thing every day after school. Henry and I went straight to the conference table and did our homework until our parents were ready to take us home. I pulled out my books and folders. I had math and Mandarin, but I wasn't in the mood. What I really wanted to do wasn't part of my usual after-school agenda.

"Hey, Henry. Who are you picking for your inventor project?" I asked.

He looked up from his homework. "That's not due until after spring break. Why are you thinking about it now?"

"I don't know. I want to pick a good one so I can impress Dr. Schwartz." Plus, I was avoiding all my other homework. I pulled out my STEM binder. A small book dropped onto the table with a thump. The cover read *The Art of Bird Watching*.

How'd this get in there?

"This isn't mine. I don't know where it came from." I showed Henry, then quickly took inventory of everything else in my backpack. All my usual stuff was there and nothing else.

"Bird watching? Yup. Definitely not yours."

I opened the book and flipped through the pages. They were

yellowed with age and made a crinkling noise when turned. Page after page was covered with diagrams, mathematical equations, and old-fashioned cursive handwriting. There was absolutely nothing about birds as far as I could tell. A torn piece of paper stuck out in the middle like a bookmark. It was bright white and contrasted with the other pages. It read, *GIVE THIS BOOK TO THE PROFESSOR*

From my study of handwriting samples, the note was scribbled in a hurry. The sentence had no punctuation, and the paper was folded haphazardly. I opened the inside cover, checking for a name or library sticker, but there was nothing like that, only an image of a sphere with the letters *N.T.* Written underneath the sphere were the words: *THE PERSONAL NOTES OF NIKOLA TESLA. KEEP IT SECRET AND PROTECT IT WITH YOUR LIFE.*

8

KEEPING IT SECRET

I suddenly pictured myself running through a field of explosions, dodging bullets and diving into a ditch to protect Tesla's notebook. This should be in a museum, NOT in my backpack!

Wait a minute. What if it was a case of mistaken identity? The note couldn't possibly be meant for *me.*

"Who would put that in your backpack?" Henry asked.

"I'm not sure. Maybe Dillon?"

Henry tutted. "You think Dillon is the cause of everything."

"Because he's sneaky and arrogant and . . ." I tried to think of the right word. "Nefarious!"

"Nefarious? What does that even mean?" Henry said. "Look, Riley, this book is ancient. I think it could be the real thing. How would Dillon even get this?"

I tried to come up with a super-intelligent observation that only a trained criminologist would make, but nothing came to me.

I flashed back to the events of the day: Dr. Schwartz's ransacked room, Dillon's thievery, Charlotte's first day, Beef Wellington for lunch. One slightly credible thought entered my brain. I had left my backpack and invention project in Dr. Schwartz's classroom when I ran to get the principal. She was always talking about Nikola Tesla like they were old college buddies and spent holidays together. She knew everything about him.

Even a not-so-trained investigator could put those two clues together. She was the only person who could have written that note, even if the writer didn't use punctuation, which was completely out of character for a teacher. Dr. Schwartz was the only logical explanation.

"It has to be Dr. Schwartz," I said. "Someone tore her classroom apart looking for something. Maybe this is it."

"Or maybe it's the ghost of Nikola Tesla, telling you to protect his book with your life." Henry made his voice deep and spooky. "This is Nikola Tesla. Give this book to the professor. It has all my secret inventions."

"Very funny."

"Seriously, Riley, you think some nutcase is looking for this book, so Dr. Schwartz put it in your backpack?" Henry raised an eyebrow. As usual, he was spot on with his skepticism.

"Well, okay, but who would think to look in a kid's backpack? It was a good strategy," I said, trying to convince myself.

We gently flipped through the pages, stopping to read a passage.

"... I can tell you that I look forward with absolute confidence to sending messages through the earth without any wires. I have also great hopes of transmitting electric force in the same way without waste."

"Wireless electricity. That's what Dr. Schwartz told us Tesla was working on," Henry said.

A thought came to me, but it felt like it originated from my gut, not my brain. "Maybe wireless electricity was also what Dr. Schwartz was working on. That's her life's work, and someone wants her to cease and desist."

Footsteps alerted my reflexes, and I slammed the book shut.

"Bird watching? I didn't know you were interested in birds." Mom stepped into the conference room. She was a bird fanatic. She even got permission from our landlord to put feeders outside our kitchen window. She ended up providing food for all the woodland creatures. I had given them names until it got out of hand.

"Oh no, not me. Birds? No. It's for school." I leaned over the book but decided not to conceal it completely. That would make me look guilty.

"We got an email earlier about an incident at your school," Mom said.

Henry and I waited. *Was there more bad news or was this the same incident we knew about?* I wondered.

"A teacher's classroom was vandalized?" she asked.

"Oh, yeah, Dr. Schwartz's classroom," I said.

"Your STEM teacher? That's terrible. I never thought something like that would happen at Washington Prep. I know it's an old building, but they take security very seriously. I don't see how anyone could break in without being noticed."

"Did the email say anything else? Anything about our teacher?" I asked, hoping for information about Dr. Schwartz.

"No, just that the problem has been resolved and they're installing more security equipment over spring break." She furrowed her brow. "Why? What happened to your teacher?"

"Oh, nothing. I feel bad for her, that's all," I said as nonchalantly as possible. What I really hoped was that she was safe from the people who wanted to kill her.

"Well, we can pack up and head home soon. I have to make one more call." Mom returned to her desk.

I nudged Henry. "Did you hear that? Mom said they take security very seriously. This must've been an inside job. Who would take a chance of breaking into a school with top-notch security?"

"That doesn't mean it was Dillon." Henry shook his head. "Don't you think you should tell someone about the strange book in your backpack?"

"That's not exactly keeping it a secret." I jabbed at those exact words written inside the cover.

Henry leaned on the table with his arms crossed. "The

best thing to do would be to contact Dr. Schwartz and ask her. Maybe you can send her an email."

I gulped. "She won't answer. I mean, she can't answer."

"Why not?"

I looked around the room to make sure no one was within earshot. "She's missing."

"What?!"

"*Shhhh*, they might've found her already. The police were looking for her. Mom said the incident had been resolved, remember?"

Henry stared at my non-bird book. "Riley, if this book can help them find her, we need to tell our parents and the police."

I hesitated. Why was I hesitating? Telling our parents made the most sense and was the most responsible solution. I pictured the desperate look on Dr. Schwartz's face when she said, "I need to trust you."

Part of me—okay, a lot of me—wanted this investigation all to myself. A real-life mystery had fallen into my lap, and this was my chance to prove myself.

"Riley. Earth to Riley." Henry stared at me.

"Let me think about it tonight, okay? If I don't come up with any other logical solution as to why this book was in my backpack, we'll tell our parents in the morning. I want to help Dr. Schwartz without breaking my promise any more than I already have. She trusts me."

Mom came around the corner. "Okay, Riley. Let's go home so I can make dinner. I'm starved."

Saved by the dinner bell. Henry couldn't argue with me anymore. I placed Tesla's notebook in my backpack and threw the strap over my shoulder. "I'll talk to you tomorrow," I said.

Henry nodded an extra small nod. *Wait, did he even nod at all?* That wasn't like him. I zeroed in on his eyes. "I'll see you in the morning, okay?" I finally got it—the Henry nod.

9

NEXT STOP–HOME

Was keeping a secret the same as lying? I guessed that since lying made you not trust someone, then keeping a secret from them would have the same effect. If I knew Henry was keeping a secret from me, I would feel betrayed. It would feel the same as if he told a bold-faced lie. I knew we were keeping secrets from our parents. I hoped they'd still trust us when we told them the truth.

I wasn't ready to confess about Tesla's notebook. Not until I figured out why I had to protect it with my life. I wanted everyone to say, "Riley, you're amazing! What would we do without you?" I wanted bragging rights like everyone else at my school who was related to someone famous or important. Except that this would be for something I did myself.

Mom and I hoofed it to the train station in the rain, sharing a small umbrella built for one. Spring had officially started, and the sky had sprung a giant leak, as if water had been waiting up in the clouds all winter and couldn't hold on any longer.

I swung my backpack around so that it became a front-pack protected by the umbrella. Tesla's ancient notebook was far more important than my skin. The book had survived decades, and I needed it to survive until I could put it into the hands of this professor person, whoever that was.

I regretted that decision when the cold rain slid off the umbrella and dripped down my back. I was soaked down to my socks. We grabbed seats on the train and Mom closed her eyes, seeming to release the tension of the day. Then her eyes shot back open. "Riley, I almost forgot. How did your invention project go?" she asked.

Did she have to bring that up? "Terrible!"

"Why? What happened?"

"You know Dillon Walker?"

"Sure. Senator Walker's son. He's kind of . . . not so nice, right?" she asked.

"Yeah, well, he stole my invention idea."

"What? How?"

"He didn't admit it, but he hinted that he overheard me talking about my lie detector pen." That was all the evidence I had. Not much to go on.

She pursed her lips tight. "I'm going to march right down there and talk to the principal about this."

I was glad she was boiling mad, but I didn't want her interfering.

"I need proof, Mom. How am I going to prove it was my idea first?" I crossed my arms over my backpack. I was cold and wet on the outside, but anger was heating me up on the inside, like a volcano about to erupt.

"There's no way there could be two lie detector pens in the same class. Your idea was unique," Mom said.

"I know, but that's not real evidence. I can't prove he didn't think of it first, or that it wasn't some kind of crazy fluke," I huffed. "I've got this, Mom. I'm working on a way to bust him." At least I would be once I had time to contemplate my next move. Dr. Schwartz's disappearance had diverted my attention.

Mom shook her head. "Well, Senator Walker can be a bit of a bully on the Senate floor. Like father, like son, I suppose."

Why should we have to put up with the Walkers just because Dillon's father was a senator? "Senator this, Secretary that. I'm sick of that school. I'm the only charity case, and everyone knows it."

"You're not a charity case, sweetie. You're as smart as any kid there. Smarter than most, actually," Mom said. "That's why you got a scholarship."

"Being smart doesn't have anything to do with it. I'm the only one at that school who isn't part of some super high-powered political family and . . ." I stopped. I didn't need to say we couldn't afford it. We had plenty of evidence of that. The school called it a scholarship, but I knew Senator Marino pulled some strings. If it weren't for Henry and Dr. Schwartz, that school would be absolutely unbearable. I wanted to fit in and feel that I was as important as everyone else.

Mom sighed. "I get it, Riley. Trust me. I hear about their expensive cars and lavish vacations all the time. But you have as much right to be at Washington Prep as anyone. They don't require parents to be elected officials or work in the White House."

Mom didn't understand. She *couldn't* understand because I didn't tell her everything that went on at school. I wasn't keeping secrets; I just didn't share things she couldn't do anything about.

Like the time I needed a viola to be in the orchestra. Mom and I weren't poor, but we were on a single-parent income, or, as Mom liked to call it, an "as-needed spending plan." A viola was certainly not a necessity in life. Then one day, my teacher happened to have a new one lying around. It was an unbelievable coincidence—*emphasis on unbelievable.*

"*Voilà!* Here's your viola," my teacher sang as she gave me my new instrument. It was so shiny, and when I slid the bow across the strings, it sounded like I actually knew how to play. But the notes turned sour when I overheard Valerie say it was a handout because her family donated the viola to the school. I never said thank you. I couldn't bring myself to say it.

"Why can't I go to the local public school in Alexandria like I used to?" I asked.

Mom put her hand on my rain-soaked shoulder. "We'll see. Maybe when you get to high school, you can go closer to home," she said.

At least that was something to look forward to, but my

glimpse into a happier future rebounded right back to the present. Now I felt like an ungrateful kid. I didn't want to make Mom feel bad. She worked really hard. Senator Marino was always bragging about Mom and saying, "I couldn't do it without her." I wasn't sure what "it" was, but maybe he could upgrade her title to something that sounded more important, like Administrative Engineer.

I decided it was best to change the subject. "A new girl started school today," I said.

"Really? What's she like?"

"She's from a small town in southern Georgia. I forget the name, but she says, 'I'm fixin' to', and stuff like that." I giggled just thinking about her, but not in a making-fun kind of way. She was the happiest person I'd ever met.

"I bet she feels a little out of place around here."

"Yeah, but her mother is the new secretary of agriculture, so she'll fit right in."

Mom looked at me sideways. "Dad never cared about those things, and you shouldn't either. Be proud of who you are."

"I know, Mom." I stared out the window like there was something to look at other than a cement wall speeding by.

I often wondered what life would be like if Dad were still alive. I'd probably be going to the local public school with kids who were more like me. Instead, Mom transferred me to Washington Prep so I could be closer to her work. Everyone knew why I was there. It was like I wore a T-shirt that said, GIRL WITH A DEAD DAD COMING THROUGH.

But that was four years ago, and Mom and I were doing fine.

"What's her name?" Mom asked.

"Who?"

"The new girl."

"Oh, Charlotte Mae Harris," I said.

"Maybe you could ask her to come over or even have a sleepover one night."

"Maybe." I tried to picture Charlotte's reaction when I asked her to spend the night. It made me smile. I'd better be careful. She might actually explode with excitement.

10

THE WATER OF DOOM

As soon as I got home, I went straight to my room and changed into warm, dry clothes. I turned on the computer and it whined and whirled as it warmed up. I carefully pulled out Tesla's notebook that was disguised as a bird-watching book. Why was it wearing a disguise and what was so monumentally important about it that I had to protect it with my life?

I flipped the pages.

This discovery means that electrical effects of unlimited intensity and power can be produced, so that not only can energy be transmitted for all practical purposes to any terrestrial distance, but even effects of cosmic magnitude may be created.

Terrestrial? Cosmic? I had no idea what it all meant, but it sounded critically important. If I were going to protect his book, I would have to act calm and do some serious lying. I'd have to learn not to fidget, stutter, or blurt things out. I might even have to use the lie detector pen on myself. This was going to be really hard.

Maybe Henry was right. We should take the book to the police. I looked at the photo of Dad on my desk. What would he tell me to do with the book? Would he want me to bring it to the police or follow through with the vague instructions on the note? There was a reason the book was given to me. I was entrusted with a mission, maybe even destined to find the truth. Hopefully, he would agree. But for some reason, I felt the need to move Dad's picture onto a faraway shelf.

My computer finally sputtered to life.

"Riley, dinner's ready," Mom hollered from the kitchen.

"Can I eat in here? I have a lot of homework to do."

I settled into the seat at my desk and studied Tesla's book again. The drawings were so elaborate and precise. One picture of a giant tower appeared several times.

Instantly, Mom appeared at the door with a plate of spaghetti. "Dinner!"

I jumped up and knocked over my water bottle.

The top shot off and water sprayed like a hose onto my keyboard.

I yanked it off the desk and turned the keyboard upside down on my bedspread.

"Ooh, ah, ee!" Mom shouted as she held the dinner plate. That wasn't helping.

I dabbed the keyboard with my bedspread as if it were a towel and peeked over at the desk.

The water had careened in the other direction, soaking Tesla's notebook. *That water was possessed.*

"Oh no, your bird book!" Mom cried.

She put down the dinner plate and grabbed Tesla's notebook.

I dropped the keyboard on my bed.

"I got it, Mom!" I quickly grabbed the notebook from her and wrapped it in a T-shirt lying on the floor.

"You really have to make more noise when you come into a room. You scared me," I said. Plus, that notebook made me as jumpy as a hardened criminal surrounded by a SWAT team.

"Sorry, sweetie. I was just bringing you dinner. Is your book okay?" Mom asked.

"Yeah, it's fine." I wasn't sure it *was* fine, but I didn't want her examining it any closer.

"Well, let me know if I can help." She paused, waiting for an answer. "I'll leave your dinner here. I'm going to go watch the news."

"Thanks," I said, then flopped back on the bed. Were all moms that quiet? Our apartment was old, with hardwood floors that creaked and doorknobs that rattled. You'd think it would've warned me she was coming.

I opened the T-shirt and felt the top of Tesla's book. The cover and first few pages were damp. *No!* . . . I dashed into the bathroom, put my blow dryer on the lowest setting and waved it in front of the book. Mom used this trick on my homework once when it fell into a puddle. The warm wind flipped the pages.

In a few minutes, the paper started to dry, but it was getting that rippled look. The cover was peeling apart like two thin pieces of cardboard that had been glued together and started to come loose.

It would never look the same. I had ruined a national treasure!

Just when I thought it couldn't get any worse, a little piece of paper shot out of the book onto the floor. Now the book *was* falling apart!

I turned off the blow dryer and picked up the paper. It was folded in half and yellowed like the rest of the book. I carefully opened it and immediately recognized Tesla's handwriting.

To whomever comes into possession of this book. In it are my discoveries that are of the utmost importance to humanity. While I failed in my final endeavor, the scientific man does not aim at an immediate result.

My work is like that of a planter. It is my hope that someone will grow the seed of my idea. Therefore, I have stored the secret to my greatest invention in a safe location where it may be found at a time when society is more willing to accept it.

I stood frozen, trying to compute this new information. Now it seemed even Tesla's secret book had secrets.

I had to talk to Dr. Schwartz and get some answers if I was going to get any sleep tonight. I pulled up the school website. The only contact for her was an email address. I typed away, hoping she checked email on her phone. And that she had her phone, wherever she was. I had so many questions.

Did *she* put the notebook in my backpack?

Was someone trying to steal it?

Who was this professor person?

Most importantly, I hoped she was all right and ceasing and desisting her life's work . . . at least for now.

I examined the first few pages of Tesla's notebook. The handwriting had faded in spots, but it was still visible. I'd only had it for a few hours, and I'd already damaged it. How was I going to protect the book with my life? I couldn't even supervise a banana in a fruit bowl.

11

DON'T TELL ANYONE

The next morning, the bell rang to start first period, and we had no teacher—no Dr. Schwartz, no substitute, no anybody. The chatter in the class grew louder by the minute. The other kids had no idea our STEM teacher's life had been threatened and she'd mysteriously disappeared. She never replied to my email. Her wrecked classroom was still under lock and key, so I couldn't get inside to examine the evidence.

Henry had texted this morning, and said he would be late today. I wanted to see his expression when I told him about the piece of paper I had found tucked inside Tesla's notebook.

"Hey there, Riley!" Charlotte shouted like a cheerleader.

"Oh, hi," I said quietly, hoping that would be a way to get her to lower her voice.

"Are you ready to finish presenting your invention?" she asked almost as loudly. "I'd really like to see how it works."

"Um, sure," I said with fake enthusiasm. My invention, which had been so critically important yesterday, was now secondary to finding the meaning of Tesla's secret message.

"I'm sure you'll do great." She opened her backpack and pulled out a sparkly covered notebook and placed it in the middle of her desk, making sure it was equidistant from all sides. *I can respect that.* Then she pulled out a matching sparkly pencil and placed it next to her notebook. She adjusted herself in her seat and sat up perfectly straight with her hands on her lap. She had impeccable posture.

She turned to me. "You look nervous," she said. "Is everything all right?"

Now I was starting to get annoyed. How did she know I was nervous? If she could read people that well, she would make a much better investigator than I would.

"N-n-nervous? Me? No," I stammered.

"Are you sure? I'm a great listener if you want to talk." She sang the last few words.

I wasn't sure about listening, but she had plenty to say and might blab about the whole thing.

I checked around the room for Henry. He was still nowhere to be found. Charlotte seemed honest and trustworthy. She had jumped to my side when I told her about Dillon stealing my invention. I could use a partner, in case I needed backup . . . or a witness. *Gulp.* "Okay, I'll tell you, but you can't tell anyone or I might die."

She giggled as if I was exaggerating.

I didn't move a muscle, so she stopped.

"I promise, Riley," she pleaded. "I know we just met, but I'm the best keeper of secrets ever. I'm like a human vault, a locked diary, a —"

I cut her off before she could come up with any more similes.

"Listen, Dr. Schwartz's classroom was vandalized yesterday morning. I think the people who did it were looking for something, and Dr. Schwartz put it in my backpack for safe-keeping."

Or maybe I really was spending too much time at the Spy Museum. . . .

"Wait. So, she didn't trip and fall?" Charlotte looked confused and a little hurt.

"No. Sorry. I had to tell you that because I was sworn to secrecy."

"What did she put in your backpack?" She gasped and her eyes lit up. "A flash drive, a key to a safe, a locket—"

"No, no, listen. It's an old book." I covertly pulled Tesla's notebook out of my backpack and opened it so she could read the inside cover and the note. I repeated the instructions to myself: *Give this book to the professor.* I kept a constant check over both shoulders for spying eyes. How was I ever going to find this person with so little to go on?

"Dang. This is the personal notebook of Nikola Tesla, the famous inventor? This could be worth millions," Charlotte whispered.

"Millions?"

"Yep. Look at these drawings and equations. This book might tell you how to build some secret invention." She nodded. "I could see why someone would be willing to kill for it."

"Kill for it?" She wasn't helping at all. She made this whole thing sound like the chilling plot to a spy novel.

"But it looks like it got wet. See how the pages are rippled? It might not be worth as much because it's slightly damaged."

Thanks for pointing that out. "Yeah, yeah, I know."

I tucked the book inside my backpack as Principal Chen walked into the classroom. Now was my chance to get an update on Dr. Schwartz. I jumped up and tripped over two desks as I stumbled to the front of the classroom.

"Dr. Chen," I whispered. "Did the police find Dr. Schwartz?"

He nodded. "Yes, she went to her sister's farm in Western Maryland."

I let out the breath I didn't realize I was holding. "That's a relief."

Dr. Chen didn't look one bit relieved.

"Did something else happen?"

He checked his phone, avoiding my question. "Riley, it's critical you don't tell anyone where Dr. Schwartz went. Even the slightest hint of rumors or media coverage could put her in danger. Do you understand?"

"Yes, I understand." I understood I had messed up already. I instantly regretted telling Henry and Charlotte anything at all. I needed to keep my mouth shut if I was going to help

Dr. Schwartz. I didn't want to put anyone in danger, including myself. I trudged back to my desk.

"What was that all about?" Charlotte asked.

"Nothing. Don't say anything about the notebook, okay?"

She nodded.

12

ADDING UP CLUES

"Students, please take your seats." The principal clapped his hands together. "We have a special guest speaker today while Dr. Schwartz is out at, ah . . . at the, ah . . . at a family thing."

I was comforted by the fact that Dr. Chen was an absolutely horrible liar.

"This is Dr. Marcus Smith. He's an inventor of many high-tech devices as well as apps you most likely have on your phones. He's donated millions to bring technology to third-world countries, and he lectures all over the world on the future of engineering. He is going to speak to you today about careers in electrical engineering."

Everyone sat up straighter.

Our guest was a tall man with a clean-cut beard. He was dressed in a rugged outfit that made him look more like an archeologist than an engineer.

"Thank you, Dr. Chen." He turned to the class. "I see you've been working on inventions of your own. There are many innovative ideas on display around the room." He motioned to our Invention Convention projects that were placed on shelves in the back of the class. "Dr. Schwartz must be very proud of her students."

If a class could glow collectively, we did.

"Let me ask you, who here is interested in a career in electrical engineering?" Several students raised their hands. "Are there any students who think it's boring?" A few more raised their hands. He laughed.

"Well, let me see if I can change your minds. Did you know there was a war about how to distribute electricity? Don't answer that, because I'm going to tell you. It was the *war of the currents*." His voice was deep and dramatic like he was about to tell a ghost story.

"Two great minds were on the quest to light up the world— Thomas Edison and Nikola Tesla."

Wait, what? Did he say Nikola Tesla? My mouth dropped open. It was like Tesla's ghost was tapping me on the shoulder and wouldn't leave me alone.

"Edison was already famous for inventing the phonograph when Tesla came from Europe to work for him in New York City. At first, he and Tesla had great admiration for each other. Tesla was a hard worker, putting in many hours without much pay. But ultimately, the two men disagreed on the method for distributing power. Tesla was in favor of his alternating current method while Edison was already committed to using direct current."

Dr. Chen jumped in. "Like the band AC/DC," he said as if he'd added something cool. He looked around at a bunch of blank faces.

"Yes, Dr. Chen, that's exactly right. The band named itself after the electrical currents," Dr. Smith explained. There were still a bunch of blank faces in the room. "I'm not sure these kids listen to AC/DC."

"Okay, I'll leave now. Looks like you have this under control," Dr. Chen said, pretending he was playing the air guitar as he left the class. *How embarrassing. But I have to giggle at Dr. Chen jamming out.*

"Okay, back to my story," said Dr. Smith. "Tesla eventually set out on his own and earned the backing of the Westinghouse Electric Corporation." Dr. Marcus Smith wandered around the room as he spoke. "Back in the late 1800s, many people were afraid of this new electricity coming into their homes. They thought it might cause fires. Wires were strung all over New York City." He strolled over to the light switch.

"Then, in the winter of 1888, a blizzard like none other hit New York." He made whistling noises and flicked the lights on and off, on and off, then shut them off completely. The room was almost black except for sunlight coming in through a small window.

Students giggled at his dramatic presentation. "The storm plunged the city into darkness. The unsightly electrical wires littered the streets." He turned the classroom lights back on. "A poor boy skipping along the sidewalk decided to play with one of the downed wires. That was a deadly mistake. He was electrocuted. They called it *death by wire*." Dr. Smith paused.

"This added fuel to the war. Edison tried to convince people that the Westinghouse Electric Company with Tesla's AC system used dangerously high voltage. The competition got so heated that one of Edison's associates publicly electrocuted an elephant using Tesla's device to scare people into thinking it was unsafe. The truth was, no elephant would've survived those high voltages with either system."

"That poor elephant," said Charlotte.

"Are we going to be tested on this?" grumbled Dillon from the back of the room.

Our guest speaker ignored him.

"Ultimately, Tesla's alternating current method of transporting electricity was more efficient, cost-effective, and used fewer wires. When he lit up the Chicago World's Fair in 1893, Tesla proved to the world that his alternating current—AC—was a superior system."

I sat calmly in my chair, listening to Dr. Smith's fascinating lecture, but on the inside, I was totally freaking out. The clues about who to give the notebook to were adding up fast.

Clue number one: Dr. Smith is an expert on Nikola Tesla.

Clue number two: He knows Dr. Schwartz.

Clue number three: Dr. Smith lectures all over the world, which means he's a professor.

I leaned over to Charlotte. *"Psst.* Dr. Smith is a professor *and* an expert on Tesla."

She stared at me and thought for a second, then two, three, four seconds. Then she gasped. "You're right," she whispered, her eyes wide.

Dr. Smith stared at us intently. I wondered if he'd heard us. I sat up straight and smiled sheepishly. *That was rude of me.*

"So, class, do you think the world is done with the exploration of electricity? There's nothing else to discover, right? We can sit back and soak in the light?" He looked up at the rows of lights in the ceiling. "Wrong. There's much more to discover. For the past twenty years, I've been researching the possibility of making electricity wireless."

Clue number four: Dr. Smith is working on wireless electricity!

"Like Nikola Tesla was working on," I shouted without raising my hand. Charlotte and I exchanged knowing glances.

"Excellent, Miss . . . " He left a blank for me to fill in.

"Riley Green."

"Yes, Miss Green. Tesla was working on wireless electricity, but he never completed the experiments that would have proved his theory. If we only knew what was in his genius brain, we might be able to conquer great hurdles in electrical engineering." Dr. Smith sighed as if finding the answers were hopeless.

But it was far from hopeless. In fact, it might only be a few feet away. Tesla's notebook could shed light on everything. I felt as if the notebook was jumping around in my backpack trying to escape so it could yell, "I'm here! Tesla's secrets are in here!"

13

LOOK, NO WIRES

I had to admit, meeting Dr. Smith was either an incredible coincidence or Dr. Schwartz planned it all along. She had slipped the book into my bag yesterday so I could turn around and give it to Dr. Smith today. It all made sense.

"Excuse me." Charlotte held her hand up. "How would wireless electricity change things? Would it mean we wouldn't need all those power lines and poles everywhere?" she asked.

"Duh, Charlotte. That's what wireless means." Dillon launched that cheap shot from the back of the room like an insult arrow. I wanted to snag it out of the air and break it over my knee.

I rolled my eyes at Charlotte as if to say, "It doesn't matter. Ignore him." She looked down at her desk, clearly embarrassed.

"Actually, that's a great question. How would wireless electricity change things?" Dr. Smith pointed at Dillon.

"How about you? Have any thoughts?" he asked.

Dillon scratched his chin. "Um . . . um . . . how should I know?" he finally said. Bullseye, right between the eyes.

Dr. Smith crossed his arms. "Well, wireless electricity would change the world."

I shivered as if a little bolt of electricity had surged through me. Dr. Schwartz used to say the same thing. I thought she was talking about it like it was a pipe dream, like it was about as possible as time travel.

Clue number five: Dr. Smith and Dr. Schwartz both think wireless electricity would change the world.

Clue number six . . .

I tapped my pencil on the desk. Never mind. I'd have to come back to that one.

"If we could transport energy wirelessly, we could send electricity to the most remote locations of the world. Electric cars wouldn't have to stop to charge. We could eliminate the dangers of electrical wires. It's hard to imagine the possibilities. Wireless is the new frontier of electrical engineering."

He shot his finger into the air, and I spotted a tattoo on the inside of his arm. It was the N.T. symbol from the cover of Tesla's notebook.

That's it!

Clue number six: He has a tattoo of the N.T. symbol from the inside cover of the book!

The clues were unmistakably pointing to Dr. Smith. He was the one who was supposed to get Tesla's notebook.

He continued his lecture. "What excites me the most is being able to transport clean energy to great distances from solar farms and wind turbines."

"The oil companies wouldn't be too happy about that," I blurted out again as though we were the only two people in the room.

"You're exactly right, Miss Green. This can be a dangerous pursuit. One scientist who was experimenting with a wireless invention disappeared in the middle of the night. Some say his work threatened the powerful oil industry."

No wonder Dr. Schwartz was keeping the notebook a secret! I glanced back at Dillon, whose Texas family was deeply invested in the oil business. He glared at me through slits in his eyes. I coughed nervously and cleared my throat. I'd better get rid of this book before I developed more nervous tics.

Dr. Smith continued his lecture on possible careers in electrical engineering, and I battled shaky leg syndrome for the rest of the class period. It was always my right leg that shook, never my left.

Charlotte leaned in close. "He's got to be the guy, Riley."

"I know. I'm going to give him the book after class."

As if on cue, the bell rang, triggering a flutter in my stomach. I had to go talk to him.

"I'll see you next period," Charlotte whispered.

I took a deep breath and walked straight to the front of the room.

"Miss Green, you ask excellent questions," he said.

Clearly, this guy was intelligent and knew talent when he saw it. "Thank you, Dr. Smith," I said happily.

"Please, call me Marcus."

"Okay, Dr. Marcus, I mean, Marcus. I think I'm supposed to give you something." I took off my backpack and dug out the notebook.

"A bird book?" he asked.

"That's just the cover."

He opened the book and turned the pages like a delicate fossil that could crumble in his hands. His eyes shifted to meet mine. "Where did you get this?"

"I'm not completely sure, but I know you're supposed to have it and protect it."

He closed the book. "I think I know where this came from. I'll take good care of it, don't worry. Thank you for bringing it to me."

"You're welcome." I zipped up my backpack.

"You're a smart girl with lots of potential."

My face grew hot, and I smiled so big I think I created dimples I never had before. "Good luck with your invention," I said.

"You too. Thanks again, Riley." He held up Tesla's notebook.

I could see why Dr. Schwartz was friends with Marcus. He was intelligent . . . and charming.

14

ACTING ON A HUNCH

Not only did I complete my critical mission of delivering the notebook, but today was pizza day. *How much better could it get?* Charlotte and I rushed through the lunch line, grabbed our deliciously cheesy pizza, and took our seats.

Henry was still nowhere to be found. I couldn't wait to tell him about Marcus, but I'd have to be extra careful. I wasn't taking any chances of Dillon overhearing another one of my secrets. He probably carried around some sort of illegal recording device.

"Where is Henry? He didn't seem sick yesterday." I looked around the lunchroom and tapped my fork on my plate.

"I don't know. I haven't seen him." Charlotte looked at me like she was about to burst with anticipation. "So, tell me! How did it go with Dr. Smith? Did you give him the . . ." She peeked over her shoulder. "You know?"

"You mean Marcus?" I shrugged, hoping I wasn't blushing. "He told me to call him that."

"Oh, excuse me. How did it go with *Marcus*?" she said.

"Terrific. He was so excited to get the book."

"That's great, Riley."

"Yeah, he has a really nice smile." I blushed this time.

"I KNOW!" She giggled.

I did a double take at a boy headed toward our table. It was Henry. He looked different and older somehow.

"Where have you been?" I asked.

"I got contacts," he said, blinking rapidly.

"Why didn't you tell me?"

He cocked his head. "I don't have to tell you everything, Riley."

"Okay, fine. How do they feel?"

"They're good, but they make my eyes itch. The doctor says I'll get used to them." He put his tray on the table. "What did I miss this morning?"

"A ton of excitement!" Charlotte said. "Tell him what happened."

"I found the professor person and gave him the notebook. Well, he sort of found me. He was a guest speaker in our class."

"They brought in a professor to teach middle school?" Henry asked.

I hadn't thought about it that way. "He probably happened to be in town and Dr. Schwartz asked him for a favor." I shrugged it off. "Anyway, he knew all about Tesla and was doing research on wireless electricity, so it all worked out." I nodded to myself.

"Cool. So now you don't have to worry about it anymore." He took a big bite of pizza.

"Wrong! I still need to figure out who trashed Dr. Schwartz's classroom." That was my original goal anyway.

"Okay, superspy. Have any leads?"

"No, but I was thinking about something. You know how Dillon's dad—"

"Here we go again," Henry interrupted.

"This is serious." I glanced around the cafeteria, checking for Dillon. He was seated a couple of tables away and caught me looking. I shifted my eyes up like I was searching for someone behind him. I leaned in toward Henry and Charlotte. "Listen. Dillon's dad is not only a senator, he's in the oil business. Dillon is always bragging about how his dad is the richest man in Texas. Well, he wouldn't want wireless electricity to become a reality because then he would have to shop at normal stores like the rest of us."

"She's got a point, Henry. The guest speaker this morning said the oil companies are threatened by wireless and might kill someone over it," Charlotte said with all the drama of a reality TV show.

"He didn't say that exactly. But he did say a scientist who was working on wireless electricity went missing."

"That's ridiculous," Henry said, blinking like a broken strobe light. His eyes didn't seem to like the foreign objects he'd put in them. "The scientist might have gotten lost on a deserted island or turned into some creature like the Hulk."

"Oh, and that's not ridiculous?" I frowned. "What I was going to say was that maybe Dillon was instructed to scare Dr. Schwartz into stopping her research."

I peeked over at Dillon's table again. He was on his way out the door. *Where was that sneaky boy off to?* Probably trying to steal someone else's invention or sabotage mine.

"I'll be back in a minute." I left my favorite lunch on the table and followed Dillon into the hallway. I kept my distance and stepped lightly like a ninja ballerina. He walked toward his locker and pulled out his phone. I hid around the corner.

"I know, Dad," Dillon said. "What do you mean? I'm trying. Don't worry. I've got this." He slammed his locker shut. "Okay," he said. "Bye."

Dillon stomped toward the classroom where all the students' inventions were being kept. *I knew it.* He was going to sabotage them. I counted to five, then turned the corner to bust him. *Wham.* A brick wall jumped out in front of me.

"What the heck, Riley? Watch where you're going!" Dillon said angrily.

"Oh, sorry." *Wait. Why am I apologizing?*

"What are you doing in there? Stealing more inventions?"

"No. I was looking for someone."

"Looking for who?" I shot back.

He narrowed his eyes. "None of your business."

"How about we use my lie detector pen right now?"

He blew out a laugh that was like a burp in my face.

"Your lie detector pen? All *that* would do is squirt ink everywhere when it fell apart in my hand." He waltzed away.

That guy was such a . . . a big . . . a total . . . jerk. I huffed so loudly I was sure he heard me all the way down the hall. *Good comeback.*

15

MISTAKEN IDENTITY

I peeked into the classroom to make sure Dillon hadn't messed with my invention project.

Our inspiring guest speaker, Dr. Marcus Smith, wasn't there, but someone else was. A gray-haired gentleman stood next to the teacher's desk unpacking his briefcase. He had a badge around his neck with several pins dangling off like scout awards.

"Excuse me. Did you see a tall man dressed like he was going hiking?" I asked.

He stopped and looked up. "No, was I supposed to?"

"Um, no, he was just here a little while ago. Are you a substitute?"

"Goodness, no. I'm a historian at the Smithsonian Institution. I used to teach at the university until I got early retirement because I was teaching too theoretically. Can you believe that? Apparently, I'm not supposed to let students think for themselves. They're just supposed to spew out the information they're given."

I was sure there was more to it than that. *Would it be rude if I left?*

"Do you know how to hook up my laptop to the screen, young lady? I'm setting up a presentation for the next class."

Two guest speakers in one day? That was highly unusual.

"Yes, sir." I was stuck. My cheesy pizza would have to wait a little longer.

He mumbled under his breath while I connected his laptop. "I should be working on my research, but instead I'm at a school with kids who'd rather be playing video games than learning about the importance of wireless electricity."

"Wireless electricity?" I stopped. There was a lot of that going around today.

He looked at me from above his reading glasses. "Yes, I'm sure Dr. Schwartz taught you something about it."

"A little bit."

"Hmmm. No doubt wasting your time teaching about rocks and dinosaurs."

"That too," I said.

He took off his glasses. "Perhaps you can help me. I'm looking for someone named Riley Green."

Me? Why me? I swallowed hard. "I'm Riley Green."

"Ah, perfect. Then I won't have to carry on with this charade. I'm Professor Albert Schwartz, but everyone calls me the Professor," he said, looking right at me.

Professor? Schwartz? I scratched my head. "Do you know Dr. Schwartz, our teacher?"

"Do I know her?! She's my daughter."

"Is she okay? Where is she?" I asked.

"Yes, yes, she's fine. Just as stubborn as ever." He wrung his hands vigorously. "Dr. Schwartz has great faith in you, and I understand she gave you something extremely valuable. You've no doubt taken a peek." He wiggled his eyebrows.

I couldn't believe what he was saying. He must be confused.

"She put it in your backpack in an emergency—and a momentary lack of judgment." He mumbled that last part. "I have come to retrieve it." He put out his hand.

"Oh no." His badge was right in front of me. I shut my eyes. I didn't want to see the glaring mistake staring me in the face. The badge said, *Professor Albert Schwartz, Smithsonian Institute Scientist and Historian.*

"This can't be right. All the clues added up to Marcus," I whispered to myself.

"What are you mumbling about? You do still have the book, don't you?"

Water, I needed water. My mouth was so dry. "I—I gave it to someone else," I squeaked out.

"What?!"

"His name is Dr. Marcus Smith. He knew all about Tesla, and he's working on wireless electricity."

"Dr. Marcus Smith? I've never heard of him." The Professor

covered his mouth and stared at the ground.

"He'll give it back! We just need to find him and tell him it was all a big mistake. He might still be here." I spoke frantically fast.

He shook his head. "I'm not so sure about that. You said he knew all about Tesla?"

I nodded.

He slumped down in a chair like a kid who had just failed a test. "It's a good thing she went to shut down her laboratory."

"Her laboratory? I'm so sorry, Professor. Marcus even had an N.T. tattoo on his arm, like on the book." I threw out random details hoping something might be helpful.

"An N.T. tattoo? What kind of hippie thing is that? That doesn't mean anything."

I paced around in a circle. I was only trying to help. It wasn't entirely my fault. I had very little to go on with the sparse information on that handwritten note. "Why did she put it in my bag in the first place?" I asked, a little defensive.

"She knew she was being followed and didn't want it in her possession. She thought I could retrieve it quickly, but I just got back into town this morning."

"I'll go find Marcus. He must still be here." I turned toward the door.

"Wait!" he shouted. "Don't tell anyone else about the book if we're to have any chance of getting it back." The Professor started packing up his briefcase.

I sprinted to the principal's office. Why was I so confident

Marcus was the one who should get the book? All my clues added up, but I should've waited until he asked for it. I had just handed a priceless treasure over to a complete stranger, and now Dr. Schwartz's secret was out in the world.

I found the principal standing near the front desk. "Dr. Chen, is Marcus still here?!" I spit out the words in between breaths.

His eyes squished together. I guessed I hadn't spoken clearly enough. Before I had a chance to repeat myself, Valerie barged in behind me.

"Dr. Chen," she said, cutting me off.

"Just a minute, Valerie." He put up his first finger, which was a nice way of saying hush up.

I wasn't prepared for that. "Um, it's okay, she can go first." I didn't want her to hear what I had to say anyway.

Valerie didn't waste a millisecond. "I wanted to let you know that I'll be taking an extended spring break vacation and I would like to have my assignments in advance."

"You'll have to talk to your teachers about that," said Dr. Chen.

"I was hoping you could send them a message and collect the assignments at the front office. That way I could pick them up before I leave." She smiled like she was posing for a picture.

"No, Valerie, that's not how it works." Dr. Chen didn't budge.

"Fine," she spun around and left. *Way to go, Dr. Chen.*

"Riley, did you need something?" he asked.

"Yes, sir. Is the professor who spoke to our class this morning still here?"

"The professor?" Dr. Chen looked confused. "You mean Dr. Marcus Smith? He's an inventor, not a professor, but he left a little while ago to catch a plane back to New York."

He wasn't even a professor? I thought everyone who got a doctorate degree was either a professor or a medical doctor.

"Did you need to speak to him?" Dr. Chen asked.

"No. It's okay." I sulked.

He looked at his watch. "Shouldn't you be at lunch right now?"

"Yes, sir. I'm just not hungry." I hung my head and went straight to my next class. I didn't want to eat pizza, and I *didn't* want to run into the real professor. The book was gone, and he and Dr. Schwartz might never see it again.

16

CHANGING COURSE

Students bolted through the front doors as the final bell rang, announcing the start of spring break. Most of them were rushing off to ski in the Rockies or swim in the tropics. My spring break would consist of a few trips to the corner store and a walk in the park. I soaked up the sun that had burst out of the clouds and warmed my cheeks. I was still holding out hope that Mom and I could spend a couple days at the beach.

It didn't matter, though, because wherever I went, my worries were coming along with me. Giving Dr. Schwartz's notebook to the wrong person was a mistake not about to be fixed any time soon. Apparently, I needed to stick with creating spy gadgets and leave the subversive activity to the professionals.

I waited for Henry on the marble steps of the school.

"Hi, Riley. Ready to go?" Charlotte bounced up beside me.

Wait. What? I wanted to hit myself in the forehead, but that would give away that I had totally forgotten I'd made plans with Charlotte to go to the Spy Museum. "Sure. Absolutely," I said in a chipper voice, as if I would never have forgotten our plans. "We just have to wait for Henry."

"Okay. So, whatcha doing for spring break?" she asked.

Nothing, but I wasn't about to admit it. "Oh, I have to catch up on reading the Unsolved Mysteries series. I learn a lot about crime fighting that way."

She laughed even though I wasn't really kidding.

"My parents said we're having a 'staycation,' which means we'll do some sightseeing in between unpacking boxes. Plus, I'll have to help entertain my little brother." She rolled her eyes. "Maybe we could hang out sometime."

"Yeah, okay," I mumbled. I didn't mean to sound so unenthusiastic, but my thoughts were running in circles. An eternal loop of indecision. Should I tell her about my epic fail with the book? *Would it help?* There wasn't much I could do about it.

Henry strolled over. "Are you coming to the Spy Museum?" Charlotte asked.

"Sure, why not? We can have a spy mission competition, although Riley will probably win."

I couldn't even smile at a compliment that would usually make my teeth vulnerable to catching flies. I stared at the ground.

"What's wrong?" Henry asked. "Did Dillon do something sneaky or mean at lunch?"

I took a deep breath. I might as well spill my guts to my friends. "No, he didn't, but something else happened, and I feel like a total loser."

They waited for me to confess. "I gave Tesla's notebook to the wrong person."

"What?!" Charlotte shouted. "You weren't supposed to give it to the handsome guest speaker?"

I shook my head. "No. I was right about the notebook, though. Dr. Schwartz put it in my backpack, but I was supposed to give it to her father. He came to get it from me today. Apparently, everyone calls him the Professor, and he works at the Smithsonian."

"Oh no. That's terrible," Charlotte cried, but then she tried to cover her shock with sympathy. "I mean . . . it's not completely your fault. It was an innocent mistake."

"I guess so." Although it really was my fault, and I was really mad at myself, which was the worst kind of mad.

"So, how bad could it be? They just contact the guy and get it back," Henry said.

"I'm sure they'll try, but the Professor seemed to think it was useless. Once Marcus finds out what is in the book, he could replicate it or sell it. If that happens, it won't be a secret anymore."

"That would be a downright despicable thing to do. Marcus seemed like a respectable gentleman. I don't think he would do that." Charlotte frowned. "Why is everything a secret? I don't get it."

"Secret! The secret! I totally forgot." I dropped my backpack and pulled out the little piece of paper once hidden in the notebook. "I found this in the book last night when it got wet."

"It got wet in the rain?" Charlotte asked.

"No, it wasn't the rain. Don't ask." I handed the paper to Charlotte.

She took a minute to read it. "He stored the secret to his greatest invention," she whispered.

"What do you think it means?" Henry asked.

"I don't know, but I'm sure it's important like the rest of the book. I have to get this paper to the Professor." That little piece of paper could be my chance to redeem myself.

"What about the Spy Museum?" Charlotte asked.

"We can do that another day. I promise. Right now, we need to head to the Smithsonian. That's where the Professor works." I had newfound hope, and I was on a mission to help Dr. Schwartz.

"Okay, I'm in," Charlotte said.

I looked at Henry, my eyes pleading for him to come with us. "All right. I'll come too," he said.

Charlotte took out her phone.

"I have to text my daddy and tell him where to pick me up at five o'clock," she said. "If I'm late, he'll think I was kidnapped and have the military out huntin' for me."

"Got it. Let's go."

It was all I could do to wait even another minute.

We changed course for the Smithsonian Museum, and I breathed a little easier. At least I was doing something to fix my monumental mistake. I placed the delicate piece of paper carefully in my backpack. I had to preserve it as if it were the last snowflake of winter.

17

THE SMITHSONIAN EXPEDITION

The Smithsonian museum wasn't one destination in D.C. The Smithsonian was a network of museums with several buildings up and down the National Mall. The main office was in the Smithsonian Castle, so I thought that would be the best place to start. Finding the Professor was going to be a long shot, but maybe I'd get lucky. I was due for a little luck right now. I checked Henry's arm. Yep, his lucky orange wristband was still secured, so at least we had a shot.

When we reached the Castle, I headed straight to the information desk. A lady sat on a tall chair sorting papers. She had a warm, sunny smile. Her badge said *Smithsonian Information Officer* like she was some kind of knowledge police.

"Excuse me. Do you know where we can find the Professor?" I asked.

"The professor? Which one? We have several." She typed

into her computer, her fingers dancing over the keys.

"Professor Schwartz. He does research on wireless electricity."

"Ah, I see. Do you have an appointment? He doesn't like to be disturbed when he's doing research." She leaned over the desk. "He can be a little . . . grumpy."

Yeah, I picked up on that during our first meeting at school. Still, I got the feeling he was just passionate about his work.

"No, we don't have an appointment, but we're students of his daughter." She examined us like she might actually ask to see our report cards.

"The Professor has a lot of students, honey. Both past and present." She went back to shuffling papers, and her sunny smile experienced a solar eclipse.

Charlotte moved in front of me and politely cleared her throat. "Ahem. Excuse me, ma'am. I promise we wouldn't bother the Professor unless it was very important. My mother is the newly appointed secretary of agriculture, and she's a friend of the Professor's."

She looked up. "Secretary Harris is your mother? Well, of course. I'm sure he'd see you, then."

We were in. But it wasn't because of luck. It was because of my friend's important connections. If I were by myself, that lady would've dismissed me like Pluto had been dismissed as a planet. I knew how poor Pluto felt.

We followed the information officer through the lobby and past red velvet ropes indicating we were entering a restricted area. I tried to copy Charlotte's perfect posture and purposeful walk. I didn't usually think about *how* I walked. Mom said I looked like someone who was just trying to get from one place to another. *What other kind of walking was there? Charlotte's, I guess.*

The information officer knocked on the door. "Good luck," she said, then took off for the lobby. *Coward.*

We waited.

No answer.

We stared at each other.

Nothing.

The doorknob jiggled.

My stomach churned.

The Professor opened the door. "What are you kids doing here? You can't interrupt my research. I could be on the verge of a breakthrough. Don't you have video games to play?"

"I found something that might help with the notebook." I pulled Tesla's secret paper out of my backpack.

He scowled like he was sure it would be a complete waste of his precious time. But as soon as he read the words, his face softened. "Where did you get this?" He held it up to the light as if it might be counterfeit.

"I found it tucked inside the cover of the notebook. It fell out when I was blow-drying it."

"You were *blow-drying* it?" His eyes flashed like headlights.

"Well, yes. Water spilled on it."

"It got wet?!"

"A little. I'm sorry. It was an accident."

He mumbled to himself. "Secret invention. Stored in a safe location." His voice lifted. "This is amazing. This could be the answer she's been searching for!"

I hoped he was referring to Dr. Schwartz. "What does it mean?"

"I have no idea, but my daughter will know." He motioned for us to follow him through a heavy wooden door and down a narrow hallway. We continued into a small office with one dirty window and an assortment of chairs.

"What is it that you do for the Smithsonian, Professor?" Charlotte asked.

"I am the curator of all things in the Technological Revolution between the years 1870 through 1914."

The Professor's office was a mishmash of historical knickknacks, piles of papers, and stacks of books on the verge of tipping over. If I didn't know better, I'd think his office had been ransacked, but I was pretty sure everything was exactly where he wanted it.

He sat down, removed his glasses, and rubbed his eyes. The Professor looked like someone who hadn't slept in days.

"The Technological Revolution was the first time that electricity and telecommunications were used in a practical way. We have thousands of papers and objects cataloged." He leaned on the desk. "But there was one object I found that was too significant and dangerous to be made public."

"Tesla's notebook." I swallowed hard. My stomach twisted

in knots as I remembered my failed attempt at protecting the notebook.

"Precisely." The Professor nodded.

"Where did you find it?" Charlotte asked.

"Well." The Professor drummed his fingers on the desk. "Let's just say it's a family heirloom. Not my family, someone else's family. And . . . I, uh . . . found it in their estate sale."

He waved his hands around like he was dusting away that minor detail. "But that's not important. What is important is Tesla's wireless electricity invention. It would greatly enhance the world's ability to transport clean energy, but it has to be developed with great care and secrecy."

"Why so secret?" Charlotte asked, a little put out. Clearly, she didn't like secrets.

"If someone figures out the invention, they could . . ." He stared at us like he'd just remembered we were kids. "Let's just say they could build it for the wrong reasons. It's our duty to develop this invention carefully and in secret until it can be protected and only used for the right reasons—the reasons Tesla intended."

He sat back in his well-worn office chair and held up the little piece of paper from the notebook. "Does anyone else know about this?"

"No, sir. I had forgotten about it when I gave the book to Marcus."

"Good, good." He spun around and stared out the window. "I'm just a historian. My daughter is the genius. She's very close to replicating Tesla's vision. The notebook is by no means a road map, but it gets you on the right track." He turned back around. "This could be the missing piece of the puzzle, the mustard on the hot dog, the pepperoni on the pizza!"

"But if the book was so secret, how could someone else know what Dr. Schwartz was working on?" Henry asked.

The Professor sighed so big I saw his chest rise and fall. "That might be my fault. Our computers were hacked a few weeks ago. The people who are looking for the lost notebook could've seen the papers I wrote about Tesla's last inventions, although they were never published."

"So the culprit could be someone who doesn't want wireless electricity to be invented?" I asked.

"That's a possibility, or they want to sell the invention for millions of dollars or millions of yuan or rubles or any other form of international currency."

The Professor's cell phone rang like an old-fashioned phone. "Hello . . . what's wrong . . . those despicable vermin . . . how could they do that?"

18

ADJECTIVE: TALL;
NOUN: KNUCKLEHEAD

Listening to a one-sided conversation was like filling in the blanks of a Mad Lib except it wasn't funny. My imagination was inserting all kinds of horrible adjectives.

"Your students are here," he said into the cell phone. "Yes, yes, they stopped by today. Riley discovered something you might be interested in." The Professor tapped the speaker button and placed his phone on the desk.

"I'm so sorry, Dr. Schwartz. I thought Marcus was a friend of yours. I'm a complete idiot. You can give me an F if you want. I deserve it." I couldn't speak fast enough.

"Slow down, Riley," Dr. Schwartz said patiently. "The Professor told me what happened, and I completely understand the confusion. It's my fault. I panicked. I shouldn't have put you in that position. But listen, the important thing now is to find the book. Do you know anything else about Marcus?"

"No, only that he lives in New York. I made the mistake of assuming he was a professor."

"Dr. Schwartz, where are you now?" asked Henry.

"I'm at my lab on the family farm, or what was my lab. I came straight here from Washington Prep to secure it." She paused. "Last night there was a fire in the barn where I keep all my equipment. I was only allowed to go back inside a little while ago." Her voice cracked. "Everything was destroyed."

"It was obviously sabotaged! The criminals don't want you to finish your research." I was fired up.

"That's my guess too," said Dr. Schwartz.

"Don't worry about the lab," her father said. "You're smart. You can rebuild it. I'm just glad you're safe."

"It's the money, Dad. Where am I going to get the money?"

We looked at each other in uncomfortable silence. I'd never heard Dr. Schwartz use that frustrated tone before. She was always so calm in her classroom. Charlotte sat on the edge of her seat but stayed quiet. That was probably very hard for her.

The Professor cleared his throat. "Well, Riley found something that might help." He nodded for me to go ahead and explain the secret paper hidden in the notebook.

I told her everything.

The phone went quiet.

I twiddled my thumbs at a breakneck pace.

A few long seconds went by. "Hello? Are you still there, Dr. Schwartz?"

"Yes, I'm here. That's incredible, Riley," she said.

I was relieved and thrilled. It was like getting an A on a test that I thought I had bombed.

"Do you know what the message means?" Henry asked.

"It means there's more of Tesla's invention to be discovered. More than what's in his notebook."

"Do you really think it's hidden somewhere?" I asked.

"I suppose it could be, but it was so long ago. It might've been accidentally destroyed by now," she said.

"Or on purpose," I added.

Dr. Schwartz continued to think out loud. "If his secret invention was in an actual place, maybe it could be at his old laboratory in Colorado Springs . . . or at Wardenclyffe in New York." She paused. "I wish there was more to the message."

Now she knew how I felt about vague notes. I didn't hold it against her.

If anyone knew where to find the secret, it would be Dr. Schwartz and the Professor. They'd been studying Tesla longer than anyone.

"Will you be able to continue your research?" Charlotte asked.

"I suppose so. I've got everything memorized. It will just take a long time, and I was so close." Her voice trailed off, then came back with a vengeance. "We need to get the book back so it's secured. Do you know when Dr. Marcus Smith left the school?"

"He left about lunchtime. Dr. Chen said he was catching a

flight back to New York," I said. "We can go find him. We can help!"

"No, no. It's okay. You've done enough, Riley. Thank you for bringing this to us. We'll take it from here."

I hung my head. They should've put a tracer on the book or put it in a briefcase and chained it to an armed guard. I hated this helpless kid feeling. If I were an adult, I could go look for it myself.

Charlotte pointed to the clock on the wall. "We have to get going," she whispered.

"Thank you for bringing this information to us," the Professor said.

"Yes, we would never have discovered it without you," added Dr. Schwartz.

I nodded. "Sorry again . . . about everything."

We got up to leave and I spotted a book on the Professor's shelf. The title was *Prodigal Genius: The Life of Nikola Tesla* by John J. O'Neill. "Professor, may I borrow this book?"

"Sure, go ahead. It's a fascinating read. Now, off you go. I've got work to do." The Professor shooed us out the door.

"Thank you for seeing us," said Charlotte.

My heart sank for Dr. Schwartz. Did she have to be so nice about everything? I'd feel better if she was fuming mad. I deserved an F. My brief undercover assignment was a total fail.

19

UNUSUAL ACTIVITY DETECTED

I wasn't a big fan of group projects. Most of the time, assignments were easier if I did them myself. There was always that one kid in the group who didn't do anything but still got the same grade as everyone else. Of course, you couldn't say anything because then you weren't a team player.

This time was different. I needed Henry and Charlotte on my team to help me salvage this investigation. There was too much at stake. I was glad they'd shown an interest so far. I hoped they realized that it had, in fact, become a group project.

"I can't believe Dr. Schwartz is really a high-tech inventor doing secret research. What on earth was she doing teaching sixth grade?" Charlotte asked.

I shrugged. "Maybe it was the perfect cover."

"I hope she can continue her research. It would be awful if she had to quit chasing her dream." Charlotte sighed.

Thanks for that. I knew Charlotte didn't mean to make me feel bad, but I already felt like I had burst Dr. Schwartz's bubble, stomped on it, and squished it into the ground.

"On the bright side, it's spring break and we don't have school!" Henry said with an irritating bounce in his step.

Charlotte pointed to a tree. "And look, the cherry blossoms are blooming!" she said.

It was nice that they were trying to cheer me up, but it wasn't working.

"Yep," I said, creeping along. I hardly looked up the entire way back to our parents' office.

When we reached Senator Marino's door, Henry grabbed the handle and pulled. "It's locked."

"That's weird. It's never locked." I knocked loudly.

"They wouldn't have left without us," Henry said.

Mom opened the door. "Hi, kids. Come on in," she said.

As soon as we stepped inside, a man in a black business suit stood up from the conference table. "Thank you, Senator Marino. We'll let you know what we find out." He marched out the front door. My suspicion radar detected unusual activity.

"Why was the door locked?" I asked.

"We were having a meeting." Mom nodded her head toward Charlotte and smiled.

Oops. I'd forgotten to introduce my new friend. "This is Charlotte Harris. She's the new student I told you about."

"Welcome, Charlotte," Mom said.

"It's very nice to meet you, Ms. Green." They shook hands.

Senator Marino introduced himself. "I'm Henry's dad, Senator Marino. I've already met your mother. She's got quite a job ahead of her." They shook hands too.

"How are you adjusting to life in D.C.?" Mom asked.

Charlotte took a deep breath and blew it out. "It sure is a big city. I'm not sure I'll ever get used to the hustle and bustle. My hometown is so small, you couldn't have the hiccups without everyone knowing about it."

Mom let out a polite laugh, or was it a nervous laugh? Something about the office was not right. It was entirely too quiet. "Where is everyone?" I asked.

"Yeah, it's like a ghost town in here." Henry had also picked up on the eerie emptiness.

"Well . . . it, ah . . . it turned out to be such a beautiful day." Senator Marino gazed out the window. "I, um, er, let them go home early."

He stammered and avoided eye contact—two subtle hints of false statements. I jotted a mental note in my noggin.

"Can we go too?" Henry asked.

"Not yet. We're waiting for Oscar to escort us," Mom said.

"Why? Did someone get fired and go berserk or something?" I asked.

"No, nothing like that," she said.

"Dad, what is it? What's going on?" Henry asked.

Senator Marino put his hands in his pockets. "I don't want you to worry, but some criminals hacked our computer system, and they sent a message," he said.

"What did it say?" I asked. "Was it a threat?"

Senator Marino looked at me like I had psychic ability. "Yes, it was. But it's probably nothing. The FBI is just being extra-cautious."

"The FBI? Dad, what did it say?" Henry pressed.

"It said, 'Cease and desist.'"

Bad omens seemed to be following us around. "Did it say, 'or die'?" I asked.

20

HAREBRAINED THEORY

Mom's eyes bulged out and her eyebrows shot straight up. "Riley, how did you know what the message said?"

"Dr. Schwartz got the same message on her whiteboard."

"Your teacher got a death threat? The school left out that little detail in their email yesterday." Her lips pressed together so hard her raspberry lipstick completely disappeared. "I think that was an important piece of information they should've shared with the parents."

Senator Marino sat down in a chair, his fingers in prayer position pressed against his lips. "Why would they threaten a schoolteacher with the same message?"

"Who are *they* and what do they want you to cease and desist doing?" Henry asked.

"The message warned me to stop new legislation to fund alternative energy sources or there would be consequences."

"Like death." *Did I say that out loud?*

"Riley," Mom scolded. *Yes, I guess I did.*

Charlotte stayed quiet, taking it all in.

"I'm the chair of the Energy and Power Subcommittee and I'm working on the new energy bill. Apparently, they don't like my plan and want me to cease and desist working on it. That's the only explanation we have right now."

"I'm just throwing this out there, but could the threat be from someone in the oil industry who doesn't want you to fund clean energy sources? You know, because it might hurt their business?" I asked. *Please say yes.*

"We can't be sure. Even some of the oil companies can see the benefit of clean-burning fuel."

"But not all oil companies, especially those who are backed by certain politicians." I'd lived in D.C. long enough to pick up on some political maneuvering.

"What are you trying to say, Riley?" Mom asked.

"That maybe there's a certain senator from Texas who is also an oil tycoon, and he wants to scare you into stopping your bill." I raised my eyebrows and Mom squished hers together. *I'll be quiet now.*

Senator Marino stared out the window. Was he actually contemplating my harebrained theory about Senator Walker?

"It's unlikely a member of Congress would go so far as to send a death threat. For one thing, if caught, they'll go to prison—not to mention lose their job." He turned to Henry. "I think it's best if you go to New York and spend spring break with your mother. I need to stay here. I'm introducing the clean energy bill in a couple of weeks."

Henry's shoulders dropped along with his backpack. "Isn't clean energy exactly what they told you to cease and desist?" He used air quotes around the words "cease and desist." I let that one go.

"There's a lot more to the bill than funding the research and development of clean energy. It's also about protecting the environment. This bill is important, and we can't cower to bullies. If we did, they'd be running the country."

Mom looked at me sympathetically. "I'll be working next week too. Sorry, sweetie."

As if that was a surprise. I knew she would have to stay in town. The problem with Mom working for Senator Marino was that everything was critical, consequential, or historical. Or all three. There was no competing with issues that affected millions of people. I was only one person who was destined to have another boring spring break.

21

HATCHING A PLAN

Mom and Senator Marino retreated to their offices while Henry, Charlotte, and I contemplated our next move.

"Is it always this crazy around here?" Charlotte asked.

"You mean, do we always have life-or-death situations?" I fake laughed. "No."

"Sometimes it feels that way, though." Henry sulked.

Our spring break was not off to a good start. We spun around in the office chairs like teacups at an amusement park. Movement helped me think, and I had to come up with a plan.

If the people who sent those threats didn't want to advance clean energy, they might be after Tesla's book so they could destroy it. We had to get the book back from Marcus before they got to him. *But how?* I put the brakes on my chair and tipped to the right, grabbing the table to stop myself from falling over.

"Henry, what if we both go to New York? We can look for

Marcus and ask him for the book back," I suggested.

"Right, because in a city of millions of people, we're bound to run into him," he said.

"It's worth a shot," Charlotte said.

"Thank you." I nodded to my reassuring new friend.

"Come on, Henry. It'll be fun. If we don't find Marcus, at least we won't be bored." *Who knew?* Maybe I could salvage this spring break and have something to write about in the school newspaper.

"I guess so, but my house in New York isn't exactly fun."

"Why? What's wrong with your house?" Charlotte asked.

"Oh, nothing, just that my mom keeps it like a museum," he said.

"I don't think we have a choice. This isn't about going on vacation, it's about finding the notebook," I said.

Charlotte stopped her teacup chair. "Wait a second. How come you go to school here if you live in New York?"

"I have dual enrollment in New York City, but I'm mostly in D.C. Otherwise, I'd hardly ever get to see my dad," Henry said.

"So you go to school at Washington Prep sometimes and in New York other times?" she asked as though she was considering this unique school arrangement for herself.

"Yeah, although I like it in D.C. better," Henry said.

"Maybe I could come to New York too. I could watch your backs." She plopped her elbows on the table and rested her big smile in her hands.

I felt like a lousy new friend, but she couldn't go. She had a lot to learn about spying. Her colorful outfits and southern accent weren't very incognito. She might give us away.

"Um, you already helped out a lot. You got us in to see the Professor," I said. "We couldn't have done that without you."

"Right, okay." She shrugged it off, but her smile faded. "My daddy would never let me go anyway."

I didn't want to leave her out, but what could I do? What could *she* do?

"Maybe you could help me bust Dillon for stealing my invention and possibly ransacking the classroom. Do you want to spend the night tonight? We could come up with some ideas."

"Seriously? That would be amazing. I'll call my daddy right now." She didn't waste a second. She pulled out her phone and strolled away from the table. I tried not to listen, but the room was kind of small.

"Well, I know, Daddy," Charlotte said into the phone. "It's just that she's leaving on vacation and this is the only night she can do it." She covered the phone. "He wants to talk to your mama."

I jotted down Mom's cell number. I should probably go warn Mom that she was about to get an interesting phone call from a southern gentleman. *Nah, she'll be fine.*

A few minutes later, Mom walked out of her office with her bag packed. "Charlotte, I'm so glad you'll be spending the night tonight. Is pizza okay for dinner?" Mom glanced at me with a look that said, "Next time check with me first."

"Oh yes, ma'am. I love pizza."

I decided not to mention we'd had pizza for lunch. Who cared, anyway, since the whole point of Charlotte's visit was for us to come up with a way to bust Dillon.

"Hey, Mom, I think it's a good idea if I go to New York and stay at Henry's over spring break. That way, you don't have to worry about me just hanging around the house while you go to work." I kicked Henry under the table. He straightened in his seat.

"Right, we can do some sightseeing," he said.

Mom cocked her head to one side. "I leave you kids for five minutes, and you've come up with all kinds of plans."

"What's going on?" Senator Marino joined us in the lobby.

Henry spoke up first. "Dad, can Riley come to New York with me? She's going to be really bored at home next week."

"Let me check with your mother. If it's okay with her, then Riley is welcome to spend spring break in New York." He smiled at Mom.

"I suppose you could do some sightseeing for a few days, but I want you home before the weekend," Mom said.

"All right, then," said Senator Marino. "We'll confirm the arrangements and get back to you."

Our security guard, Oscar, poked his head inside the front door. "Everyone ready to go?"

"Yes, thank you," Mom said.

Oscar led the way down the hall, and we followed like little ducklings.

I wished I was more excited about actually going somewhere

on spring break. But it was like someone shook an ice-cold can of Fanta and I couldn't drink it, or it would explode in my face. The fact that someone threatened Senator Marino meant Mom was in potential danger too. At least Henry had to admit this was more serious than he'd thought. He had to get involved now because it just got personal.

22

ALL ICING AND NO CAKE

After dinner, Charlotte and I collapsed on the floor in my room. Mom had set up a blow-up mattress next to my bed. I turned on my big, clunky computer so we could do some online espionage.

"Wow. What is that?" Charlotte asked.

"It's a very old computer." I laughed. My big boxy screen attached to a computer tower with tangled wires dangling behind the desk was definitely an eyesore. "I pieced it together from Mom's hand-me-downs over the years."

"I've never seen one like that before—well, except in the movies. Does it still *work*?"

"Sure, I just wish it had a faster processor. I'm saving up for a laptop." I wasn't really, but I had just realized that was probably a good idea.

Charlotte stood up and strolled around my room, exploring

the trinkets and books on my shelves. "So, do you really think Dillon's daddy might have something to do with the cease-and-desist messages?"

"I don't know, but I overheard Dillon talking to his dad on the phone today, and he sounded angry."

"Maybe Dillon told his daddy about the wireless electricity discussions we had in class today," she said.

"Yeah, and Senator Walker wants it to stop, like banning books in the library." I spoke in an imaginary Senator Walker voice and wagged my finger in the air. "There will be no more lessons about wireless hocus pocus at school!"

Charlotte laughed.

My computer finally perked up and was ready to go to work. I typed "Senator Walker" into a search engine hoping to find a mug shot with a row of numbers underneath. No such luck, but I did find something else.

"Hey, Charlotte, there's an article here that says Senator Walker is up for reelection this year."

"That's it!" she said. "I bet a lot of oil companies contribute to his campaign and he wants to show them he can defeat the clean energy bill. I can find out who donated to him."

"You can? How?"

"It's public record, plus I have my sources." She winked, but she needed more practice in the art of winking. The entire left side of her face scrunched up. It was more of a mouth wink.

Charlotte picked up a picture frame. "Is this your daddy in the police uniform?"

"Yeah. He died a long time ago." I threw that out there so quick, it sounded like I didn't care, but I did care—a lot. I just didn't want anyone feeling sorry for me. I held my breath, waiting for a sympathetic comment oozing with forced sincerity. Charlotte didn't attempt one. I was relieved.

"What happened to your daddy?" She placed the photo down.

"He and his partner were the first ones to respond to a hostage situation. His partner went around to a back entrance when my dad got shot." I turned to face Charlotte. "The weird thing is, the guy who took the hostage never made any demands. No one knows what he wanted, and they never caught him either." I stared at Dad's picture. "One of these days, I'm going to find out what really happened."

"Did the hostage survive?" she asked.

"Yes. She's a really nice lady. I've met her a couple times."

"So your daddy's a hero." Charlotte smiled.

"You can say that." I had a warm feeling inside, like when someone unexpectedly remembers your birthday.

"I bet he was a great police officer if he was suspicious like you," she said.

"You think I'm suspicious?"

"You sure are. You like to solve crimes and bust liars. Think about it, Riley. You invented a pen that detects lies. That's amazing! How did you code a program to work with the pen?"

"I did it in my Girls Who Code club. You should join," I said.

"I don't know. I reckon I could give it a try."

Charlotte had only known me a couple of days, but it was like she had seen a movie trailer about my life and got all the highlights.

"How do you like Washington Prep so far?" I asked her, hoping she would say it was awful.

"It's fine. Way more exciting than my old school." She giggled.

"Yeah, I guess so." I shrugged with a frown I couldn't hide.

"Why? Don't you like it there?"

"It's just that the kids are kind of snobby and hung up on status and stuff." *There I go again.* I said too much. Now I sounded like a whiner.

"I can see that. My old school was the same way. Who's the captain of the football team? Who's in the Miss Tifton Pageant?"

I cracked up. "Yep, that's kind of like Washington Prep. There's an unspoken ranking of kids."

"You mean like a pecking order in a henhouse? My nana says to ignore all that. It's just a bunch of chicken poop. She says people who care about that stuff are all icing and no cake."

I think I'd like Charlotte's nana.

I guessed I could try to ignore the henhouse, but keeping my mouth shut from complaining about school would take a surgical procedure.

Charlotte reclined on the blow-up mattress. "To be honest, if I were forced to use your lie detector pen, I'd have to write, 'I feel like an alligator in the Arctic in this place.'"

Quick, Riley, think of something helpful and encouraging. How could I make her feel better if I felt out of place myself?

"You'll get used to it. You just moved here," I said.

"I suppose so, but I know some people are talking about me behind my back," she said. "They're making fun of my accent. I can't help it. It's how I talk."

"I like your accent," I said.

"Maybe I could change it to something else . . . like British." She sat up. "Blimey, Riley, I'm having a smashing good time. Brilliant, I say." She sounded like a southern belle in a Harry Potter movie.

"That was the worst British accent I've ever heard." I laughed so hard I couldn't breathe. She joined in, and we giggled like lifelong friends.

"I have an idea," I said. "How about I be your permanent tour guide? I'll show you all around D.C. so you know it like a local. The first thing we'll do when I get back from New York is go to the Spy Museum."

"That'd be great," she said. "And if you find Marcus, I'm sure he'll give the book back. He seemed really nice."

Right. The notebook. For one brief moment, I'd almost forgotten I was on a critical mission to save Dr. Schwartz's life's work. There was no way I could come back from New York empty-handed and sit in her classroom like I hadn't lost her most precious possession. I'd feel like I was the chicken at the bottom of the pecking order. No, I'd feel like the poop lying on the bottom of the cage.

23

NEW YORK, HERE WE COME

I'd always wanted to go to New York and explore the city, but now I was having serious second thoughts about my daring detective adventure. I wasn't prepared to find Marcus. I didn't have any spy gear, fingerprint analysis kits, or hidden cameras. I didn't even have high-powered personal connections like Charlotte. All I had was my school backpack and a suitcase filled with clothes for each day of the week. That was as prepared as I could get.

Henry's mom greeted us when we got off the plane at LaGuardia Airport. "Hi, kids. You two look a wreck. Did you sleep in those clothes? We'll get you fed and washed up as soon as we get home." Henry rolled his eyes but managed to do it with a smile.

When we reached the car, I sank into the plush leather seats in the back of Mrs. Marino's BMW. As soon as we took off, I hung on for dear life. She sure knew how to swerve through traffic. Mrs. Marino drove with one hand on the wheel and the other on the horn. I wondered if she'd honk at a bug if it dared to splat on her windshield.

"We're getting ready for the big fundraising dinner at our house, so there's plenty of food," she said. "Your father will be here for that tomorrow."

"Do I have to go?" Henry asked.

"Yes, your father is up for reelection this year. You have to at least say hello to everyone. You know, make the rounds, small talk, and all that."

"How long do I have to stay?" Henry asked.

"A couple hours and then you can go play your video games." Mrs. Marino glanced in the rearview mirror. "You can come too, dear."

"Thanks, but I didn't bring anything fancy to wear."

"That's okay. My personal assistant, Randall, will find something. He's an expert at that."

Henry glanced back with an apologetic smile.

"Thank you. That sounds like fun," I said.

After we got off the highway, I gazed out the window at the sidewalks crammed with people walking, talking, and looking at their phones. None of them were staring up at the tall buildings like I was.

I couldn't help looking for Marcus among the faces on the streets, even if finding him was as likely as finding a needle on Planet Haystack. What would I say if I actually ran into him—"Hi, Marcus, remember me? I'm the one who gave you Tesla's notebook. Well, you probably know that it's a very rare, priceless artifact that could hold the secret to creating unlimited energy. Yeah, can I have that back?"

* * *

Henry's house was a flurry of activity; glasses clinked, pots clanked, and the vacuum hummed. As soon as we walked in, a man wearing stylish, urban clothes and holding a clipboard hurried over. "Is that Henry? My, how you've grown! And you got contacts!" he said.

"Yeah. Hi," Henry mumbled.

"And who is this?" Randall took my hand. "With your height and beautiful hair, you could be a model."

I felt my ears get warm and my face turn red. "Right, that's my fallback plan in case my crime-fighting inventions don't work out."

He laughed politely. "Mrs. Marino told me you need a dress for the fundraiser. I'll find the perfect one for you. I know the perfect little shop."

He'd said "perfect" twice. His expectations were entirely too high. I was sure to break several rules of etiquette during the night. I hoped I didn't burp, trip, or get anything stuck in my teeth.

Henry cleared his throat. "Well, we have some research to do for our STEM project."

"Okay, sweetie. Carry your bags upstairs. Riley can take the guest room on the right. Please clean up after yourselves."

We headed up the main staircase. Henry opened the door to a large bedroom clearly meant for distinguished guests, not a regular kid like me. Heavy antique furniture filled the room along with the scent of candles and clean linens. The bed looked like a giant marshmallow, with every pillow flawlessly fluffed.

"It's very . . . elegant," I said.

Henry shrugged. "Yep. I'm gonna drop off my bag."

I kept up with him so I could take a peek inside his room. I was curious to see what it would tell me about him. He opened the door, and it looked like a picture from a catalog—spotless, with no clothes or junk lying around. This definitely wasn't Henry.

"Nice room," I said.

"Yeah, I'm not allowed to touch anything, though."

I hoped he was exaggerating.

"I'll meet you back downstairs. I'm going to get changed," he said.

"Okay." I started down the steps but stopped toward the top when I overheard Mrs. Marino talking in a hushed tone.

"Henry is such a nice young man," said Randall.

"Thank you. He's a little shy, but he'll eventually grow out of it. Look at his dad." She laughed. "Don't tell anyone, but he's being groomed to be president someday. At least that's my plan."

President? Henry? I tried to picture him in the Oval Office signing important documents and standing behind a podium giving inspirational speeches. Actually, he'd make a great president. I wasn't sure he wanted the job, though.

Henry's heavy footsteps clomped down the stairs, and the conversation stopped. "Come on, let's go to the study," he said, passing me on the steps.

I followed behind, gazing around at the high ceilings and stunning artwork on the walls. Being in Henry's house made me feel as though I had to act a certain way and be a different person. The house itself seemed to have expectations. I could see why Henry preferred to stay with his dad at their D.C. apartment. Henry could be himself there—the Henry I knew.

24

THE MISSING NOTEBOOK

The Marinos' study was as majestic as the rest of the house, with bookshelves from floor to ceiling and a stone fireplace in the center. I noticed some happy family photos in pretty frames spread around the room. Maybe Henry's mom was a little wound up about her husband's election, but with any luck that would be a temporary situation.

I walked with my hands in my pockets as if I were in a real museum and didn't want to break anything.

Henry sat down at an antique wooden desk and turned on a laptop. "Where should we start?"

"Do a search for *Marcus Smith in New York*."

He typed away at the keys. "Well, this isn't good. There are 791 Marcus Smiths in New York alone."

"That's not going to work. What if we try typing *Nikola Tesla's notebook*? Maybe it will show up for sale somewhere."

I laughed sheepishly. We wouldn't be able to afford it anyway.

Henry pressed enter and a few options popped up on the screen. "Take notes. Maybe I'll do my report on Tesla," he said.

"Wait a minute. What if I want to do my report on Tesla?" I was certain Dr. Schwartz would be impressed with that.

"I thought you wanted to do your project on some lady from the Spy Museum."

"Well, I haven't decided yet. Tesla is still an option," I argued.

"Fine, we can both do our papers on Tesla so take notes. My mom expects As." His voice trailed off. "Bs and Cs make her grumpy."

"Don't worry. We'll get to the report. I promise. Keep typing!"

Henry poked at the keys and then clicked on an article. "Here's one called 'Tesla's Remarkable Papers.'"

Nikola Tesla died of natural causes in 1943 at the age of 86. He lived at the Hotel New Yorker, where a maid found him passed away. Immediately following the inventor's death, Mr. Tesla's nephew, Sava Kosanovic, hurried to the hotel room. When he arrived, his uncle's body had already been removed, and his safe had been opened. Mr. Kosanovic claimed that technical papers were missing along with a notebook that contained hundreds of pages of his latest work and inventions, including wireless electricity and the death ray. These papers and the notebook were never recovered.

I leaped out of my seat as if a spider had landed on my head. "I lost Tesla's notebook! The book they thought was lost but wasn't lost, and now really is lost!"

"Calm down, Riley. We have to think. This isn't helping." Henry bit his fingernails.

"What do you suggest we do?" I grabbed a pen off the desk and clicked it in and out, in and out. *Tesla was working on the death ray?* That sounded like something out of an old black-and-white movie where the evil mastermind threatens to use his genius invention to take over the world.

Henry quickly scanned the computer screen. "Look at this." He waved me over. "It's the Free Energy Blog."

"Anything about Dr. Marcus Smith?" *Click-click, click-click.*

Henry tutted. "Would you please stop that?"

"Did you tut at me?"

"Yes. Enough with the clicking," he said.

"Sorry." I placed the pen on the desk. No, that wouldn't work. Too tempting. I opened the drawer and dropped it inside.

"Look at this symbol. Isn't it the same N.T. as the one on the notebook?" he asked.

"Yep, and the tattoo on Marcus's arm."

Henry stopped. "Really? He had it tattooed?"

"Right here." I pointed to the spot where Marcus had the N.T. tattoo on his arm as Henry's mom walked into the room.

"Who on earth would make such an irresponsible decision?" she snapped.

I froze. *Me. I would. I'm irresponsible.* But how did she know?

"Hold on a minute," said Mrs. Marino.

She turned to Henry. "Kids, I need to straighten up in here. Why don't you head upstairs? It's getting late."

My whole body relaxed. Mrs. Marino was on the phone talking about some other irresponsible person.

"Okay, I'll shut down the computer," said Henry.

Mrs. Marino continued her phone conversation.

I leaned in next to Henry. "I know this sounds crazy, but I can't just sit around here and do nothing. I want to go look for Marcus Smith and get that book back. That's what I came to do," I said.

Henry stared at the floor, which was what he always did when he had to make tough decisions. *What was it about the ground that helped him think?* I kept my mouth shut and let him do his mental exercise.

"Okay, we can keep working on it tomorrow, but let's go to the library. We need to stay out of Mom's way while she gets ready for her dinner."

"Thanks, Henry."

He shrugged. "It's worth a shot."

We were doing the right thing by keeping our search for the notebook a secret. I was pretty sure. Not entirely sure, but that would have to be good enough for now. Dr. Schwartz needed that book to continue with her invention. It wasn't like she was working on the death ray . . . *was she?*

25

SEARCHING FOR SECRETS

The next morning, Henry and I took the subway to the Mid-Manhattan branch of the New York Public Library. He knew the subway system like a local, and I got a glimpse of how Charlotte must feel trying to find her way around D.C. This time I was the tourist, tagging along in a new, unfamiliar city.

The sidewalks were packed with people rushing in front of each other. I scoped out hidden corners looking for suspicious characters. If I were a real investigator, I'd have to have eyes in the back of my head to catch criminals. *Wait.* That gave me the idea for another crime-fighting invention—a tiny camera you pin on your back so you can watch everything behind you on your cell phone. Like a back-up camera for your clothes.

We raced up the steps of the library and went straight to the children's section. Henry pulled out his laptop, and I pulled out *The Life of Nikola Tesla* book I got from the Professor's office.

It was well-worn, with lots of underlined sections, earmarked pages, and notes written in the margins.

Henry's eyes were fixed on the screen while mine scanned the room to find all the possible exit routes as a precautionary measure.

"Riley, look at this." He turned his laptop toward me. "I did a search on wireless electricity and a bunch of entries came up."

"Wow, there are a lot of people trying to figure out Tesla's wireless invention," I said.

"Yeah, it's like a race to see who can be first."

"Wait, what's that?" I pointed to a listing specific to Tesla.

Henry scrolled through the pages of a blog.

"It's called the Tesla Foundation. It's a group of researchers and historians. They study Tesla's theories and promote his inventions," he said.

"Are there any pictures? Maybe Marcus is part of the group." I didn't want to say so to Henry, but Marcus's chiseled features were quite memorable.

"There, that's him!" I pointed at a photo of Marcus in front of an old warehouse with a caption that said, *Nikola Tesla's Wardenclyffe Laboratory in Shoreham, New York.* He was surrounded by other researchers. "Is there a way to contact him?" I asked.

"Not directly. There's just an email for the Tesla Foundation."

"Well, move over." I nudged Henry and plopped down in his chair. I clicked on the link. My fingers couldn't type fast enough.

My name is Riley Green and I'm looking for Dr. Marcus Smith. I made a big mistake and gave him something I wasn't supposed to, and I really need it back. We're here in New York and I can be reached at 555-354-2412. My sincere apologies for this random request and any inconvenience this may cause the foundation. BTW, I'm a huge Tesla fan.

Riley Green

I hit the send button before I could change my mind. I'd laid on the desperation a little thick, but it was a long shot anyway. "Come on, let's find some books on Tesla while we're here. Maybe there will be some information about this Wardenclyffe Laboratory."

"You think you can find Tesla's secret invention at that Wardenclyffe place, don't you?" he asked.

"What? No, of course not!" I said, all defensive. "Okay, maybe."

26

LIBRARY DUDE

The library had several floors lined with rows and rows of books. We entered the expansive atrium and felt overwhelmed, so we made a beeline for the reference desk.

A husky guy with a ponytail and several colorful tattoos sat behind a computer. He wore tiny glasses that looked too small for his head, and his giant fingers typed gently on the keyboard as if he were a concert pianist.

"Excuse me, do you know where we can find books about Nikola Tesla, the inventor? We have to write a report for school," I said.

"Oh, totally, this is Tesla town," he said, smacking his gum. *Smacking his gum?* I thought chewing gum in a library carried a prison sentence.

Library Dude jumped up and appeared even more Herculean. We followed him up two flights in a hurry. Even with my long legs, I had a hard time keeping up. He darted through the stacks, knowing exactly where to go. "I've studied Tesla for years. Did you know he used to do research at the library across the street?"

"He did?!" Henry and I said at the same time, sounding way too loud for a library.

We gazed out the window. "Yep, the Bryant Park area was his old stomping grounds." Library Dude stopped at a shelf in the nonfiction section and brushed the spines of the books with his fingers. "Here's a good one," he said, handing me a heavy hardcover.

"Some people say Tesla was crazy in his old age because he talked about extraterrestrials and the ability to project his thoughts onto a screen." Library Dude snapped his gum. "Still, he had about three hundred patents and would've had more if only he had written down his invention ideas. Tesla depended on his incredible memory to preserve them in secrecy." He turned back and scanned the books again.

I had kept my lie detector pen a secret too, or at least I thought I had. That was probably not the best idea. If I had told more people about my pen, they would know I had been working on it before Dillon. Instead, he was able to steal my idea and would probably steal the show on convention day. How could he get away with that? It was thievery, like walking off with a Picasso painting from an art museum. He had stolen my intellectual property, and I wasn't sure how much of that I had left.

"Tesla is an inspiration to many people." Library Dude tapped his head with his finger. "I have a few wacky ideas myself, but do people call me crazy?" He shook his head. "Don't answer that."

I giggled but stopped when my sixth sense kicked into overdrive. I had a feeling someone was listening to our conversation.

I looked to my left.

There was no one.

I peeked through a gap between books.

Sure enough, a guy with a blue baseball hat was on the other side of the shelves. He was turning the pages of a book entirely too fast to be able to read them. Maybe he was a Tesla fan and wanted to listen . . . or maybe he wasn't. *Brilliant deduction, Riley.*

I dug out my phone so I could take an inconspicuous picture. By the time I fumbled around in my backpack, he was gone. It was probably nothing anyway.

I turned my attention back to Library Dude, who was in full Tesla historian mode. "If you want to know some real juicy stuff, check out the FBI file about his death. Here's a book that has the actual documents. Some of the good parts are redacted, so we'll never know what really happened." He leaned over so he could whisper, and I got a whiff of his fruity gum. "When Tesla died, the Office of Alien Property seized all his personal papers. It was during World War II, and they didn't want his inventions to fall into enemy hands . . ." He looked around as if spies were watching us now. I appreciated his suspicious nature.

"Even though the U.S. and Russia were allies against Germany, there was no trust between us. Both countries were pursuing powerful weapons."

"You really know a lot about Tesla," said Henry with admiration in his voice.

"He was an interesting guy." Library Dude looked fondly out the window. "He used to spend a lot of time at Bryant Park feeding the pigeons. He never married, so in his final years he found friendship with those pesky little birds." One pigeon landed on the windowsill and stared at us like it was looking for his friend Nikola. "He's not here, little guy, he's long gone," said Library Dude.

Henry and I exchanged glances thinking the same thing— Library Dude was a little strange.

"Well, thanks for the books. We really appreciate it," I said.

"Glad to help," he said. "By the way, if you want to check out any of these books, come see me. Kids aren't supposed to check out adult books, but if you promise to take good care of them and return them on time, I'll let you check them out."

"Awesome. Thank you," said Henry.

"Good luck with your research." Library Dude headed back to the reference desk.

We went straight to the children's section and got to work. I scanned the pages of one of the books and stopped at a story about the Nobel Prize. "Listen to this," I whispered. "Tesla turned down the Nobel Prize for physics in 1912."

"What? Maybe he was a little crazy," said Henry.

"Well, it says here it was to be a shared award with Thomas Edison."

"Shared? I didn't know they could do that."

I read the passage aloud so only Henry could hear. "'Tesla believed there was a distinction between being an inventor of useful appliances and the discoverer of new principles. He declared himself a discoverer and Edison an inventor. He thought putting the two of them in the same category was insulting to his accomplishments.'"

"That sounds about right," Henry said.

"Maybe one day Dr. Schwartz will win the Nobel Prize!" I said too loudly and was shushed immediately. I sank in my seat, but I couldn't help getting a little excited for Dr. Schwartz. If she could find Tesla's secret invention, she would be on her way. Then Dr. Schwartz would be a true discoverer, and I would be her discoverer apprentice.

27

ROTTEN LUCK

We stayed in the library until Henry's stomach demanded food, which seemed to happen quite often.

"Are you hungry? I'm hungry," said Henry. "Come on, we can get something from a food stand near the park." He shut his laptop and placed it in his backpack. Library Dude checked out our books and we headed outside. The park was lively with people enjoying springtime in New York. We ordered sandwiches and grabbed a table near the cafe.

Out of the corner of my eye, I spotted someone running toward us. My flight instincts turned to fight. I spun around in karate position—not that I knew karate, but I'd seen some on TV. It was Dillon! Of all the people we could bump into in one of the biggest cities on the planet.

"What are you guys doing here?" he demanded without even a greeting.

"Don't scare us like that. What are *you* doing here?" I asked right back.

"We're on vacation. *Phff.* Some vacation. It feels more like a field trip. All we've done is go sightseeing. Dad says I have to visit more of America if I want to be president someday."

"You? President?"

"Yeah. I could be president," Dillon said. "What are you two nerds doing here during spring break anyway?" Dillon glanced down at my *Prodigal Genius* book. I casually placed my elbow on the cover.

"We were . . . um." I scanned the park, searching for ideas. "We were going to ride the carousel and . . . play on the putting green." I scratched my nose. I really had to get better at lying.

"That's lame. You came all the way up here to do that? It looks to me like you're working on your inventor project," Dillon said. "I was going to do my project on Tesla, but my dad said he was a nutcase."

My blood boiled and I tried to think of a comeback. *Something smart. Something bold.* "No, he wasn't!" I shot back, failing at both smart and bold.

Dillon turned and spotted his family. "I gotta go. Maybe I'll run into you guys later. You never can be too sure where I'll show up next." He laughed and hurried away.

Henry returned to his sandwich as if Dillon hadn't just been here ruining our day. He was clearly better than I was at letting things go. I supposed I could work on that, but Dillon could spoil the fun quicker than a power outage at a video game party.

I closed my eyes and relaxed my balled-up fists so blood could rush back into my fingers.

When I opened my eyes, the man in the blue baseball hat was sitting on a nearby bench, reading a book. Dillon had distracted me from my usual suspicious observations. I had a gut feeling we were being followed. I remembered Dr. Schwartz saying she had the same feeling in the days leading up to her classroom being destroyed. Mom always said I was like Dad in a lot of ways—other than being tall. Maybe I also got my highly developed sixth sense from him.

Baseball hat man caught me staring, jumped up, and waved down a taxi.

"What are you looking at?" Henry asked.

"See that guy getting into a cab?" I pointed at the car. "I could've sworn he was watching us in the library."

Henry looked at him. "Well, he's gone now, so hopefully it was nothing."

I shook it off too. It was probably my overactive imagination setting me on edge again.

Henry opened his backpack. His face creased with concern.

"What's the matter?" I asked.

"This is weird." He pulled out a small cardboard box. "This isn't mine."

"Be careful. It's a suspicious package," I said, half joking, but then stopped. That wasn't funny. Now it was Henry's turn to have a strange object snuck into his backpack.

Henry held the box out in front of him. We walked over

to the lawn and placed it on the grass, away from people, then stared at it like it might perform a trick.

"I'm really curious about what's inside, but I'm a little afraid to open it. Are you?" I asked Henry.

"A little. Maybe we can poke it with a stick." Henry dashed around a couple of trees.

I checked the box for markings. It was completely blank. I slowly peeled back a piece of tape holding the lid closed.

Henry ran back with a thin stick about a foot long. "This was all I could find." He poked at the lid until he got enough leverage to flip it open. Finally, the top flew up and we jumped back.

Nothing happened except us looking jumpy and paranoid. We laughed, letting all the tension escape like water from a hose.

"It's birdseed!" I picked up the box and ran my fingers through the tiny seeds, spilling some in the grass. A small piece of paper rose to the top. I pulled it out.

This couldn't be right.

There must be a mistake.

We were just kids.

I passed the paper to Henry. It read, *CEASE AND DESIST OR DIE.*

28

A ROUGH DAY

I threw down the box of seeds. Within seconds, a frenzy of pigeons descended on the free food. We covered our heads and sprinted under a tree.

"Someone's following us." I panted. "Does anyone besides Dillon know we're in New York?"

"Probably. It's not a secret. I mean, I live here," Henry said.

I scanned the crowd for suspicious characters. *Who was I kidding?* This was New York City. There were too many to count.

"The criminals who are looking for Tesla's notebook know we have some kind of connection to it. We both know Dr. Schwartz and the Professor."

"Somehow they know we're looking for the notebook," said Henry.

"It might be the guy in the blue baseball hat. Maybe he saw

what I typed to the Tesla Foundation. Did we exit the screen?"

"I can't remember." Henry pointed to a police car that was parked on the street. "Look, there's the police. Let's go tell them."

"Yeah, okay." I grabbed Henry's arm, instantly changing my mind. "Wait! Tell them what?"

"Tell them we got a death threat," Henry said.

"A threat about what? A threat to stop looking for Tesla's secret notebook?" I crossed my arms and talked in a deep voice, pretending to be the police. "What's so important about this notebook? Why does someone want to kill you for it? Where are your parents? Do they know you're here?"

I raised an eyebrow. "See where I'm going with this?"

"Good point," Henry said. "Come on. Let's get to the subway."

Henry took off through the park. I followed along, checking around us, above us, and behind us with every step. The area was full of eyewitnesses who could be called to testify if something tragic happened to us. I smiled and said hello to everyone we passed, like the Wal-Mart greeter. I didn't care if I looked stupid. I wanted people to remember that tall, lanky girl who sprinted through the park with a goofy smile on her face.

We stopped at the corner of West 40th Street and Sixth Avenue. The street sign read *Nikola Tesla Corner.*

"That library guy was right. This is Tesla town. Look." I pointed to the road sign. "One of the most ingenious men in the world and he only gets a corner named after him?"

"Yeah, but he also has a really cool car company named after him." Henry looked around like an owl.

"That's true. Let me get a quick picture of the sign." I pulled out my phone and took one step back. In a flash, Henry yanked my arm and hurled me into a giant planter. All I saw was a black car racing by. I heaved myself out of the planter and looked for the car that wanted to run me over like a speed bump. It had already disappeared into heavy traffic. *How much more could my rattled nerves take?*

"It was an electric car, for sure. I hardly heard it coming," Henry said.

"Thank you. That was quick thinking."

He shrugged like it was no big deal, but it was a big deal. He'd saved my life.

"I hate to say this, Riley, but it looked like the driver was trying to hit you . . . on purpose."

Me? What did I do? I just wanted to protect an artifact and help my teacher.

"Come on, let's get out of here," Henry said.

We turned back toward the subway station, and someone else came sprinting toward us. It was Library Dude, holding a lunch bag.

"Are you okay?" he asked.

As he said that, the pain in my arm reached my brain.

"You're bleeding." Henry said, pointing at my elbow.

I turned my arm. Blood dripped toward my hand. "It's only a scratch," I said.

Library Dude dug into his bag and pulled out a napkin. "Here, use this."

I held the napkin against my elbow.

"Thanks."

"You gotta be careful or you'll get run over around here," he said.

"Did you happen to see the license plate?" I asked him.

"No, sorry. What's with the birdseed in your hair?"

"Oh, we got attacked by some pigeons." I shook my head.

"You two are having a rough day."

"The worst," Henry said.

"I see you found Tesla's Corner. The old Engineers Club is right over there, if you want to check it out. That's where Tesla used to hang out with the other cronies back in the day." Library Dude motioned to a building across the street.

"Thanks, but we have to get going," said Henry.

"Yeah, I better get a bandage for my elbow." Plus, my courage was failing.

"Here's my card if you need any more help with your Tesla project."

I took the card. It read Freddy Esposito—Librarian, Musician, Pet Psychologist and Chauffeur.

"Well, gotta run," he said. "My sandwich is getting soggy." Freddy trotted back toward the park. He was a peculiar guy but seemed genuine.

As we crossed the street, my legs wobbled from the near-death experience. My nerves weren't doing too well either.

They seemed to question whether to continue this crazy search for the notebook. *Was it worth it?* What was the worst thing that could happen if some bad guys got their grubby hands on it? They might create one of the most significant life-altering inventions in history, claim money and glory for themselves, and use their fortune to mastermind an evil empire. Yeah, we really needed to get that book back.

29

A CLEAR MOTIVE

When we arrived at Henry's house, we dodged the party planners and went straight upstairs.

"You probably want to wash that elbow. I'll get some bandages." He took off down the hall.

I tiptoed into the bathroom and turned on the faucet. I slowly dipped my elbow under the water, anticipating the sting that was sure to follow. *Ouch, ouch.* I dabbed it dry with toilet paper. I didn't want to ruin the Marinos' fancy towels.

Henry rushed back with various sizes of bandages. He carefully applied a big square one to my arm. It was strange having Henry tend to my injury. For a brief moment, he looked older, as if I had caught a little glimpse of him in the future.

"Should we tell our parents about the box we found in your backpack?" I asked. I left out the part about almost getting run over by a car.

"Yeah, but . . . let's wait until after the party," he said.

That was probably a good idea. Henry's mom seemed to be on Planet Stress. I wouldn't want her to go into orbit with this news.

"Okay, let's split up the library books so we can both do some research," I said.

Henry handed me two books. "We can compare notes later."

"Okay, I'll see you at dinner." I strolled toward the guest room but then turned back. "Hey, Henry, thanks again."

He smiled shyly and disappeared into his room. I'd always known I was lucky to have Henry as a friend, but right then, I realized just how lucky I was. He didn't have to help me recover the notebook. That was above and beyond any friendship obligation.

I hoped he felt he was a little lucky to have me as a friend too. Let's face it—sometimes I could be a little . . . overly driven and slightly impatient. *Nobody's perfect.*

I glanced over the railing to the main floor below. People rushed around like they were preparing for a visit from royalty. I was both nervous and excited. What would I talk about with a room full of adults who were prominent politicians and business leaders? I was still six years from being able to vote.

I felt a little better when I saw a beautiful crimson dress lying on the bed in the guest room. It was sleeveless and flared out at the bottom. I had never worn anything so fancy.

I closed the door and turned on the television. It was

programmed to a news channel. The reporters were discussing the "Cease and Desist or Die" threat made to Senator Marino. I jumped to the edge of the bed and turned up the volume.

NEWS ANCHOR: *Our Channel Two reporter Lisa Campbell is at the Senate office building with the latest news on the apparent death threat to Senator Marino. Good afternoon, Lisa. Has there been an update on the situation?*

REPORTER: *The FBI has declined to comment on specifics because it is still an active investigation. However, they did reveal that a second threat was sent to a teacher at Washington Preparatory Academy. The teacher's name has not been released for safety reasons.*

NEWS ANCHOR: *Have they identified a motive for these threats?*

REPORTER: *The FBI has not confirmed a motive, but Action News has learned that the message was a threat against funding alternative energy.*

NEWS ANCHOR: *Is Senator Marino still planning to move forward with the clean energy bill?*

REPORTER: *Yes, he is putting the bill up for a vote next week and, according to our sources, it's going to be a very close vote.*

I couldn't believe my ears . . . and my eyes. My theory about the death threats had been confirmed on national television. Putting an end to new sources of clean energy *was* the motive.

Senator Walker sure would like his oil business to be free of competition from other industries.

I wanted to call Mom and brag. I wanted to tell her how I knew it all along. The FBI should focus their investigation on the

Walkers. I started to text her, but I stopped. How much should I tell her? Would she start asking questions that might lead to even more questions? If I told her about the notebook and the cease-and-desist note, she'd be on the next plane to New York.

ME: *Hi, Mom.*

MOM: *Hi. Are you having fun?*

Fun? My lower lip started to tremble. I wanted to be brave, but the box of birdseed and the near-hit-and-run made me crave a big hug from Mom. I squeezed my eyes shut. I would only be here a little bit longer. I'd be home by the weekend, whether I had the book back or not. I wiped my nose with my sleeve and replied to her text.

ME: *Yep. Everything is good. We went to the park today.*

MOM: *Great. Was it nice?*

ME: *Yep. There's a party tonight.*

MOM: *I know. I bet they'll have lots of great food.*

ME: *Well, better go.*

MOM: *Have some fancy food for me. I'll call you tomorrow.*

ME: *K.*

Someday—hopefully soon—I'd tell her everything.

30

DIVISIBLE BY THREE

I collapsed on the marshmallow bed in the guest room and flipped through a library book. I stopped at a section called "Tesla's Idiosyncrasies."

Apparently, Tesla was a germaphobe and avoided shaking hands. If someone caught him off-guard and accidentally shook hands, Tesla would be so distracted that he couldn't continue the conversation until he washed his hands.

He was an impeccable dresser and purchased a new tie every week. He claimed to sleep only two hours a night. Once a year, he would sleep for five hours, which would give him a "reserve of energy."

How could anyone function on such little sleep? This was fascinating. I turned the page.

Tesla requested two dozen cloth napkins at every meal and polished his silverware many times before throwing the napkins on the floor. If a fly landed anywhere on the table, he insisted the entire meal start over.

Tesla had high expectations for his assistants and could be difficult to work with, but he was very generous with wages and tips.

He liked things to be divisible by three, including the number of his hotel room. He lived at a few different hotels in his adult life and died at the New Yorker Hotel in room number 3327 on the thirty-third floor.

I wanted to keep reading, but my eyes felt heavy. So much had happened, and the day wasn't over yet. I lay my head on the plush pillow, and when I looked down, Tesla's notebook was no longer lost, it was in my hands. I was in the Marinos' study, turning the pages and admiring the detailed drawings. Tesla's words might as well have been written in hieroglyphics, but I tried to interpret them anyway. I crossed the room to the armchair next to the fireplace. When I approached, I tripped on an area rug in the shape of Texas. The book flew out of my hands and into the fire and instantly went up in flames.

I was jolted awake by a knock on the door.

"Riley, are you coming down to the party?" asked Henry.

Oh, no. How could I have fallen asleep? "I'll be there in a minute."

That was the worst dream ever, but I was relieved that the book hadn't been destroyed in a fire. It was just lost somewhere in New York, which seemed a little better.

I brushed my hair and teeth, threw on the dress, and forced

on shoes that were a size too small. I'd have to deal with them for one night. Besides, they made my feet look more delicate, which was no easy feat.

I rushed down the stairs. Henry and his father greeted me at the bottom.

"Hi, Riley, I'm so glad you could come to New York," said Senator Marino.

"Thank you, Senator. I'm so glad you didn't die," I blurted out loud.

"Really, Riley?" said Henry.

"I mean, you know, with the death threat and all."

"Riley, *shhh*," Henry said again.

"What?" I was still a little groggy from my nap.

Senator Marino cleared his throat. "Your mom is holding down the fort for me in D.C. I couldn't do it without her. I told her we would take good care of you."

He stopped when he noticed the bandage that didn't blend in with my fancy dress. "Oh no, what happened to your arm?"

"It's fine. I just fell on the sidewalk," I said quickly. Which wasn't a total lie.

"Let me get a picture of you and Henry." Senator Marino pointed to a spot in the foyer.

I posed next to my friend.

"You look nice." Henry grinned.

"So do you." I elbowed him. *Ouch*. Bad idea.

Henry's mom ran over to straighten his tie. She wore a sophisticated dress and smelled like a department store.

"Now Henry, stand up straight and greet everyone with a handshake," she demanded.

"I will." He squirmed in his suit.

"Smile!" she said.

31

OH, SAUSAGE BALLS

The guests arrived, and the party was quickly in full swing. Two police officers stood guard at the front doors, probably as an extra precaution because of the threat against Senator Marino. Little did they know that Henry and I were the victims of a threat as well. Hopefully, there was also an undercover agent or two milling around in the crowd.

I moseyed from room to room sampling the food and chasing down the man handing out little sausage balls and cheese puffs. Somehow food tasted better when it was shaped into spheres. I had thought the adults would ignore me, but instead they kept asking me questions: How do you like New York? What's your favorite subject in school? What do you want to be when you grow up? Some of them had never heard of a criminologist before.

After a while, my cheeks hurt from constant smiling.

I scanned the crowd for Henry. He'd managed to disappear. I didn't blame him. By now, my feet ached as if a boa constrictor were squeezing the life out of them. A big cushiony chair in a corner facing a window was calling out to me. I limped over and as I was about to plop down, I found Henry.

"What are you doing here?" I squeezed in next to him. The chair was just big enough for the two of us.

"My stomach hurts. Too many sausage balls." He burped.

I kicked off my shoes and moaned like my grandpa. *Sweet relief.* I took a deep breath and tried to relax, even though we were minus one notebook and plus one death threat.

"This wasn't the spring break you were hoping for, was it?" said Henry.

"Yeah, I was expecting skydiving and bungee jumping." I pretended to silent scream. We both laughed at that ridiculous visual.

Henry seemed as out of place in his own home as I felt at school. He lived in a luxurious house with a prestigious address but he looked like a happy meal in a gourmet restaurant. That was okay by me, because if he was a hamburger, I'd be the french fries.

He peeked over the back of the chair and put his fingers to his lips. Senator Marino stood right behind us in conversation with a woman in a royal blue dress. I really wished I had invented that back-up camera for clothing so I could see behind me.

"It's been a battle, but I think we have enough votes to pass the clean energy bill next week," Senator Marino said.

"That's good to hear because Senator Walker has been campaigning against it. He does not want this bill to pass." She cleared her throat. "For obvious reasons. If he can convince enough senators to defeat the vote, the momentum for your bill might fizzle out. But I wish you the best of luck."

Of course Senator Walker didn't want clean energy, and I bet he wanted to get rid of Tesla's notebook so it never saw the light of day. I elbowed Henry in the ribs with my good arm, a little too hard. He recoiled and mouthed, "Ouch."

Another man's voice entered the conversation behind us. "Excuse me, Senator. May I have a word?"

"Of course, Agent Garcia," he replied.

"I have some good news. My investigators have a lead on the computer hacker. The suspect is in Texas, and we're taking him in for questioning."

I opened my eyes wide. Henry covered his ribs, anticipating another blow. I gave him an I-told-you-so look. I knew it had to have something to do with Dillon's Texas tycoon family.

"That's a relief," said Senator Marino.

"Well, nothing firm yet, but we'll keep you posted."

"Thank you. I'll feel a lot better when the criminal is behind bars. At least no one else has gotten a death threat."

I felt Henry tense up, and I had a lump in my throat the size of one of those sausage balls I'd crammed in there.

32

SECRETS AMONG FRIENDS

I scooted to the edge of our big, comfy chair and turned so I could look Henry straight in the eyes.

"Did you hear what that woman said about Senator Walker? He's going to try to block your dad's bill. And the FBI agent said the suspect is in *Texas*. That's right, Texas, home of the wicked Walkers." I sat back and crossed my arms.

I knew the FBI was working on the case and had the most advanced crime-solving tools at its disposal, but that didn't seem like enough. My gut was telling me the Walkers were behind this—if not personally, then financially. If Tesla's notebook could hurt an entire industry run by wealthy, powerful people, those people would definitely want to destroy it.

Henry's phone buzzed, and he twisted in the cushiony chair to get it out of his pocket. "It's Charlotte. She's been trying to reach us."

"I left my phone in the room," I said.

"Come on. We can go to the study." Henry and I snuck around the corner into the enchanted room of books. The festive noises were muffled when we closed the heavy wooden door.

"Here. You call her." Henry shoved his phone into my hand. I tapped on her number, and Charlotte popped up on the screen. "Hi, Charlotte."

"Finally! Where have y'all been? I've been trying to reach you," she said.

"We were at a party." I placed the phone on the desk so she could see both of us.

"Wow, Riley. That's a snazzy dress. What kind of party is it?" She sounded a little jealous.

"Not a fun kind. A boring kind," Henry complained.

"Well, anything is better than playing hide and seek with my brother. One time, I didn't go find him for a half hour, but then I felt bad, so I baked him cookies."

"Cookies sound better than hanging out at this party." Henry yawned.

"I also had some time to do a little investigating, and I have some information about Dr. Marcus Smith."

"Really? That's great." I grabbed a pencil to take notes.

"He's speaking at a conference at the New Yorker Hotel tomorrow."

"How did you find that out?" Henry asked.

"Like I said, I've had tons of time to kill."

I couldn't believe it. Charlotte had come through for us again. I rapidly tapped the pencil on the desk. "We can go to the hotel tomorrow and ask him for the notebook back, right, Henry?"

"Would you stop that?" he snapped. "I can't think."

Apparently, Henry couldn't deal with my nervous tics. "What's there to think about? This is our chance to get Dr. Schwartz's notebook back!" I shoved the pencil into the drawer along with the pen I'd placed there earlier.

"I wish I could go with you," Charlotte said.

"Me too." We could use some of her sweet-talking.

"I gotta go. Mama says I need to have my room unpacked by the end of the week."

Charlotte looked behind her at the stacks of boxes, baskets, and bags of clothes. She sighed. "I'm sort of a pack rat . . . no, more like treasure keeper . . . no, I just plain hate partin' with stuff."

I laughed. "Thanks, Charlotte. I wish I could help with your room."

She leaned in so close to the phone, I could see her eyelashes. "Don't tell anyone, but I'm looking forward to school starting Monday. This has been the worst spring break ever."

"Your secret is locked in my human vault." I smiled.

"Thanks. Ya'll be safe now."

I couldn't believe my spring break wasn't as bad as Charlotte's. I guessed I'd rather be doing something than nothing at all.

We said goodbye, and I waited for Henry to say something. He was staring at the ground again.

"What's wrong?"

He took a deep breath. "I really wanted to tell our parents about the cease-and-desist note, but even if we tell them after we get the notebook back, we have nothing to show them."

That glaring mistake hit me in the gut. I paced back and forth. "I should've kept the box of birdseed and the note or at least taken a picture of them. We don't have any evidence. No proof that we actually got a death threat." What was I thinking? *Way to go, Riley Green, hopeless amateur.*

"We also can't prove you almost got run over by a car. They might say it was our imagination," Henry added.

I collapsed on a chair. We had no note with the death threat, no chance of tracing the package, and no license plate from the runaway car. We literally had nothing except the word of two kids—us. Who was going to believe our story? And even if they did, how could they track down any evidence?

"How about this? We go to the New Yorker Hotel tomorrow and get the notebook back. Then we call in the professionals, even if they don't believe our story," I said.

"Okay, one more day. Promise?" he said.

"Promise." I nodded.

"Come on, we might as well get some dessert." Henry grabbed the giant brass handle on the carved wooden door and pulled it open.

We stuck our heads out of the study. The sound of classical

music and the cackling of guests rushed back into the room. We turned the corner, and there he was. The very person we'd been looking for. I froze.

Marcus was standing right in front of me.

33

JUST ACT CASUAL

Henry slammed into my back, knocking me forward a step. "What's wrong with you? Keep moving," he said.

I stood between Henry and his dessert—not a good place to be.

"*Shhh.* It's him. It's Marcus," I muttered under my breath.

"What? Where?" I tilted my head toward the man in the pinstripe suit standing in the middle of Henry's house, the man who had Tesla's notebook, the man we'd been looking for.

"Don't stare!" I grabbed Henry's arm and dragged him back a few steps. "What should I do? Should I go talk to him?"

"Um, yeah. Isn't that what you've been wanting to do?"

Now? Why was I such a big talker? I was so nervous my mind was a blank. *Think logically.* I just had to put a series of words together in a particular order and spit them out like a printer. I wished I could print out the message, hand it to him, and run. But that would be cowardly, not confident and poised like Charlotte.

That was it! I could channel my inner Charlotte, waltz right up to Marcus in a sophisticated manner, and state my objective. I took a loud, deep breath and moved like every step was dipped in cement.

Marcus was in an animated conversation with two other men. His hands were waving around as if they were enhanced communication devices. He must have had outstanding peripheral vision because he spotted us approaching immediately. He raised his eyebrows and broadened his smile.

"Excuse me, gentlemen. I need to talk to this smart young lady," he said. "Riley, what are you doing here?"

"I'm visiting my friend Henry." I pulled Henry toward me so I could introduce him . . . and use him for moral support.

"I don't remember seeing you at Washington Prep." He put out his hand toward Henry.

"I was absent that day," Henry said, shaking hands.

"Henry is Senator Marino's son," I said.

"Ah, well, that is a wonderful coincidence." Marcus glanced around the room, then toward the front door. "I'm a big supporter of your father. After all, he holds the purse strings to funding clean energy research."

Okay, Riley, spit it out. "Marcus, I have to ask you something. Do you still have the notebook I gave you?"

"Of course. I'm protecting it." He took a sip of his drink.

"The thing is, I really need it back. I wasn't supposed to

give it to you. It's actually very dangerous to have." My hands were extra fidgety, and my fancy dress didn't have any pockets. I forced myself to clasp them behind me.

"Really? Why is that?"

"Let's just say bad things happen to people who have it," I whispered.

He leaned in close. "Is it a good idea for me to give it to you, then?"

Another punch in the gut. He was right. How was I going to answer that one? I was just a kid who couldn't protect anyone. My mind was searching for a sensible explanation when he started to laugh.

"Don't worry. Someone already beat you to it," he said.

Henry and I exchanged glances.

"Dr. Schwartz contacted me yesterday and told me about the mix-up." His voice was warm and understanding.

I let out a huge sigh, completely losing my perfect posture. "Oh, that's a relief. I'm so sorry. It was all a big mistake."

"It turns out Dr. Schwartz and I were at Columbia University together. She told me a couple of her students might be in New York looking for me. I'm just glad the notebook is safe, and no one else knows about it. Right?" He raised his eyebrows.

"Right." I nodded at Henry.

"Right," he said.

"I'm meeting Dr. Schwartz at Wardenclyffe tomorrow to give her the notebook and take her on a private tour. Not many people have access to it, but I have special privileges."

He winked. "I can't miss the chance to show her around. She's going to flip out! Just being there is so inspirational."

Marcus looked like a kid in a toy store where all the toys were free.

"How about you two come along with us? Maybe she'll give you extra credit. I'll send a car to pick you up in the morning. I insist."

"That would be amaz—"

Henry cut me off. "Riley, I don't think my parents would allow us to . . ."

I held up a finger. "Excuse us for a minute, Marcus." I pulled Henry aside.

"We're not going," Henry said. "We got a death threat too, remember? We shouldn't go."

I was the one with the super sixth sense, and I thought it would be fun. "Dr. Schwartz will be there and maybe—"

"This is not a good idea, Riley." He shook his head.

"What if we get Freddy, the Library Dude, to drive us? His business card said he's a chauffeur. Then we'll have our own car, and we can leave whenever we want."

Henry scratched his head.

"Please, Henry." I poured on the friend guilt, which actually made *me* feel guilty too. I just couldn't win.

"Okay, but only if the Library Dude drives us, and I seriously doubt he will."

I turned back to Marcus. "We can meet you there tomorrow, but we have our own ride. You don't need to send a car."

"Okay, then. Be there by ten thirty sharp. You won't regret it. But don't tell anyone about the private tour. Wardenclyffe is only open to the public twice a year." He looked at his watch and chugged his drink. "It's time for me to go. Good luck to your father. He's got my vote."

"Goodbye, and thanks for everything," I said.

Marcus pretended to tip an invisible hat. My cheeks felt hot. A great ending to another bizarre day that started out a complete disaster.

"This is so great. Can you believe it? He came to us. It was destiny. Serendipitous, I tell you!" I gave Henry a quick sideways shoulder hug.

He smiled. He couldn't argue with how great this day turned out.

"Okay, Riley, so this means Dr. Schwartz will have the notebook back tomorrow, and we can for sure tell our parents about the cease-and-desist note."

"Right. As soon as we get back from Wardenclyffe, we'll tell them. Come on, let's go get that dessert." My stomach suddenly had room for more fancy balls of food.

34

ADVICE FROM THE GRAVE

I woke early the next morning with entirely too much on my mind. Nikola Tesla had said that the scientists of today think deeply but should think more clearly. I had to think clearly.

I flipped through one of the library books, looking for clues that would tell me where Tesla's secret invention might be stored. The pages were full of photos of Tesla's laboratory and the 187-foot tower at Wardenclyffe. Apparently, people had been afraid of it. It was during World War I, and they thought it could be used as a weapon. Tesla ran out of money before he could prove his wireless theory. He had to watch his giant tower be dismantled and sold off to repay his debt. His dream of building a worldwide telegraph system vanished.

I am unwilling to accord to some small-minded and jealous individuals the satisfaction of having thwarted my effort. These men are to me nothing more than microbes of a nasty disease. My project was retarded by the laws of nature. The world was not prepared for it. It was far too ahead of time, but the same laws will prevail in the end and make it a triumphal success.

Wouldn't Tesla have wanted his theories proven eventually? *Think clearly, Riley.* He didn't want America's enemies to develop his technology. Maybe he hid his secret somewhere that wouldn't be destroyed. The little piece of paper inside Tesla's notebook was meant to guide someone to discover his earth-shattering invention . . . when the world was prepared for it.

I bounced out of bed and ran down the hall in my pajamas. I knocked on Henry's bedroom door. "Henry, Henry! You'll never guess." He cracked the door open and peered through, forcing his eyes open.

"I know where the secret is! Tesla wanted someone to figure out his invention someday and that day could be today." This revelation was coming to me fast and furious.

"Yeah, so?"

"It's at Wardenclyffe. I just know it. Hurry up and get ready. We have to go."

"Did you call Library Dude and ask if he could take us?" He was completely missing the significance again in favor of practical logistics.

I threw up my hands. "I completely forgot. I'll do that right now." I darted back to the guest room, dug out the business card, and tapped the number into my phone.

"Hello," said a groggy voice.

"Hi, Freddy. This is Riley Green. We met at the library yesterday. Remember, I almost got hit by a car?"

"Oh yeah, the Tesla investigators."

"Right. Well, we need to go somewhere important today, and I noticed on your business card that you're a chauffeur, and we were wondering if you could take us. We can pay you." That sounded pathetic.

"Today's my day off." There was silence on the other end. This was a dumb idea. There's no way he would want to drive two kids on his day off. "Where did you need to go?" he asked.

"Um . . . Wardenclyffe in Shoreham, on Long Island." I cringed, waiting for an answer.

"Really? I've always wanted to check that out. . . . Okay, then, you've got a deal," he said.

Wait, what? This plan was actually working? "Um, do you take credit cards?"

"Sure. Credit cards, green money, barter. Anything but Bitcoin."

"Can you meet us in front of the library in about thirty minutes?"

"Very well, Miss Riley," Freddy said through a yawn. "I'll see you then."

I ran back to Henry's room and knocked on the door.

He cracked it open. "What?"

"We're going with Library Dude. I mean, Freddy is taking us to Wardenclyffe."

"You're serious?"

I smiled. Henry looked at his feet as though they were talking to each other, trying to make up their minds. "All right. I'll tell my mom we're going back to Bryant Park. Meet me downstairs in ten minutes."

"Cool." If we discovered Tesla's secret, Dr. Schwartz could finish her research and win the Nobel Prize. I would be admired by the entire school. I knew that wasn't the point, but still, everyone would look up to me, and it wouldn't be because I was tall.

35

BRILLIANT DEDUCTION

A black Town Car slowed to a stop in front of the library. Freddy jumped out, ran around the car, and opened the passenger door for us like we were movie stars going to a premiere. "Good morning, Miss Riley. Your carriage to Wardenclyffe awaits."

I giggled like Charlotte and wished she were here. I was so impressed with myself for thinking of this idea, but my opinion changed as soon as the car door opened. Freddy's ride was glamorous on the outside, but a complete dump on the inside. The seats were torn, the floor was filthy, and the smell made me gag. I pulled up my shirt to cover my nose.

"Sorry about the mess back there. My passengers are typically the four-legged kind. My pet chauffeur business is booming. Most taxis won't take them."

Ohhh. I got it now. "You're a pet psychologist and *pet* chauffeur." That was not clear on the business card.

"Yep, I do a little of everything," Freddy said. "I'm still searching for my true vocation. I want to do something important. You know what I mean?"

I uncovered my nose. "Yes, I know exactly what you mean." That was why I was in this stinky car going to visit an old dilapidated warehouse.

"I've always wanted to see Wardenclyffe. How did you two rascals get permission to go? You're not pulling a flimflam, a swindle, a fast one, are you?" Freddy talked like an actor in an old detective movie.

"Hey, do you read Raymond Chandler?" I asked, pleasantly surprised.

"You betcha. I've seen all the movies too." He pulled out into traffic. "No one ever gets my obscure references, though."

"I wonder why," said Henry.

I laughed. "We're not pulling a flimflam. We're meeting our teacher at Wardenclyffe. For a . . . um . . . a field trip."

"Cool." Freddy turned on some music. "It's going to take about an hour to get there, so sit back and enjoy the ride. My playlist is a little eclectic. It's designed to calm nervous dogs."

Oddly enough, I wasn't showing any physical signs of nervousness. Going to Wardenclyffe hadn't been on my bucket list a few days ago, but now I was actually excited to go to a historical landmark on my spring break.

36

FRIENDSHIP GUILT

A large statue of the famous inventor stood at the front of Wardenclyffe as though standing guard over the property. But the wrought iron gates were wide open.

"This place looks deserted. Are you sure this is where you're supposed to meet your teacher?" Freddy asked.

"Yep. This is it. Just like the photos on the internet," I said.

Freddy stopped the car, and now I had to break the news to him. We couldn't let him come inside with us. Marcus didn't want us to tell anyone else.

"I'm sorry, Freddy, but we have to meet our teacher by ourselves. No one else is allowed to go on the tour." I made up that last part.

He sighed. "That's the life of a chauffeur. Will you take lots of pictures? I'd really like to see the inside."

"Absolutely." I stepped out of the car.

"I saw a coffee shop down the street. I'm going to get a cup of joe." He yawned. "I had a late gig last night. If I'm napping when you get back, knock on the window."

"Thanks, Freddy." I closed the door.

He pulled away, kicking up dirt on the gravel road. Henry and I stood alone, staring at the building.

"You go first," we both said.

"I'll go. It was my idea," I said with phony confidence.

From the outside, the old warehouse looked like it didn't want any visitors. Every window was boarded up, and every bush was overgrown. If the building could talk, it would shout, "GET OUT AND STAY OUT!"

Yet we kept creeping closer. Was that thinking clearly? I'd find out soon enough.

We turned the corner to the side of the warehouse. A loud metal clank echoed from inside the building.

"What was that?" Henry asked.

"Someone or something is inside."

"That's great detective work, Riley." He scanned the area. "I wish we had my smasher blaster—at least I could shoot gumballs if I needed to."

Come on, Riley. Don't chicken out now. This could be my chance to uncover one of life's biggest mysteries.

One of the boards covering a doorway had been pulled open. A stream of sunlight shined inside.

"Hello?" I called out.

"Let's take a few pictures and wait out front for Dr. Schwartz to arrive," Henry suggested.

"Yeah, good idea." I pulled out my phone as a man stepped out of the building. I took a step back.

"Riley and Henry. I thought maybe you were Dr. Schwartz." It was Marcus. He was dressed in his rugged clothes again.

"She's not here yet?" Henry asked.

"No, but she should arrive any minute. I just got a text that said she's on her way from the airport." Marcus scanned the Wardenclyffe property. "I thought you were getting a ride from someone. I don't see any cars."

"Our friend dropped us off. He went to get some coffee," I answered.

"Oh, okay. Do you want to take a peek inside? I'll save the grand tour for when Dr. Schwartz gets here, but it's really amazing." He waved us into the building.

I stepped forward, then glanced back at Henry. He wasn't moving.

"Come on, Henry. Dr. Schwartz will be here soon."

"I have a bad feeling about this. Maybe we should wait here," said Henry.

"Maybe you should trust me," I said, laying on the friend guilt again. I came all this way to make a discovery, and nothing was going to stop me—okay, a lot could stop me—but now Henry was making me question my courage. I really wanted him by my side. "Please, Henry. I don't want to go without you." That was the truth, not a guilt trip.

He finally moved his feet and followed me through the narrow opening into the expansive warehouse.

Marcus led the way. His giant flashlight revealed a high ceiling and large picture windows. "This building is more than a hundred years old," he said. "It's in disrepair, but some Tesla supporters are raising money to restore it as a museum."

We walked to a cement staircase that led to a lower level. "You have to see this." He turned to face us. "I am about to show you—" He paused, maybe for dramatic effect, then said, "Tesla's secret lab."

Secret? Lab? This could be it. I felt like an archaeologist about to discover an ancient treasure. I pictured Dr. Schwartz's astonished face when I handed her Tesla's secret. Would it be a box? A book? A key? I wasn't sure, but I was sure about the newspaper headlines—GIRL FINDS TESLA'S HIDDEN SECRET.

37

THAT DIRTY RAT

Marcus flung the strap of his flashlight over his shoulder and led the way down steep steps into a large octagonal chamber. "Tesla built an underground tunnel to run wires between the laboratory and his tower." He shined his light around.

The underground chamber was dark and cold, with cement walls and dirt floors. A pitch-black tunnel veered off into the creepy unknown. *If I were a ghost, this would be a great place to hang out with my spooky friends.*

There wasn't much else to look at—no workstations or old equipment. This couldn't be the highlight of the tour.

A faint noise came from farther down the tunnel. I moved next to Henry. *Maybe this wasn't such a good idea.*

"We really should go back upstairs so we don't miss Dr. Schwartz," I said. "You did bring the notebook, right?"

Marcus paced back and forth in front of the door. "Yeah,

about that. You see, I've been working on this wireless invention for twenty years, and every time I've come close to finishing, something goes wrong." He pretended to pull out his hair. "It's infuriating!"

His tone changed, and his friendly demeanor vanished. I checked for exits, which I had failed to do before entering the dungeon part of the tour. *That wasn't like me.*

"You were right to give me the notebook, Riley. I'm a far better engineer than your teacher." His eyes shifted toward the dark tunnel.

A garbled groan floated into the chamber.

"Thanks to Tesla's long-lost notebook, I've completed my designs for wireless electricity. Now I'm revealing *my* invention at the New Yorker Hotel today. It's fitting since that's where Tesla died. I'll be hailed as the genius inventor of wireless electricity."

"That's nice. Good luck with that." Henry grabbed my arm. "We need to get out of here, now!" We took one step toward the door, but Marcus moved in front of it. He stood between us and the staircase to freedom.

"I'd hoped to find the notebook in Dr. Schwartz's house or her classroom. Hiding it with a student was unexpected. Unfortunately, that leaves loose ends to tie up." He pointed his flashlight at us.

How could Marcus have fooled me into believing he was the good guy? *Because I am a fool, that's how.* Marcus lied about everything.

Guilt and fear tangled inside me, making a stabbing knot in my gut.

"And now Senator Walker will be implicated for sending the threats." He smiled a greedy, ugly grin.

"You *framed* Senator Walker?"

"My hackers were in Texas for a reason." He laughed too loudly for that stupid joke.

I remembered giving Henry's dad the idea that another senator wanted to squash his bill. *Did I help send the FBI in the wrong direction?*

"Someone had to cover up my search for the notebook. I couldn't just go around asking for it, now could I?" His eyes were as cold and dark as the tunnel.

"But Dr. Schwartz and the Professor know about the notebook, and there may be others." I wasn't about to mention Charlotte's name and put her in danger.

"That crazy old professor couldn't build a simple catapult. And sadly, your teacher is missing again." He pointed his flashlight to a figure slumped against a wall farther down the tunnel.

"Dr. Schwartz!" I dashed over to our teacher's side. Blood and dirt stained her forehead, and a bandanna was tied around her mouth. I pulled it down.

"You're a thief," she coughed out to Marcus. "You'll never be a great inventor." Dr. Schwartz held her arm tight against her side.

My vision blurred with tears.

"Your teacher was supposed to have died in the fire at her laboratory, but instead she came looking for the notebook. Now all evidence of the notebook will soon be buried in Tesla's tunnel. I'll be known as the greatest inventor of all time. Better than Franklin, better than Edison, and even better than Nikola Tesla." Marcus backed toward the door.

"You're not going to leave us down here. You can't—" The walls were closing in on me.

"I tried to warn you, Riley, but you just wouldn't *cease and desist.*"

Marcus turned, and Henry moved with surprising speed and leaped on his back. But Marcus shook him off like an annoying bug. Two more years of growth and he might've had a chance. Marcus kicked Henry in the chest, knocking him backward onto the floor. The heavy metal door slammed shut, sealing us in.

38

TRAPPED

I pounded on the door knowing full well Marcus wasn't coming back. "Let us out!"

We were going to be buried alive.

No one knew we were down here.

Mom would be all alone.

I should've told her everything.

I should've told the police.

I squeezed my eyes shut. Tears streamed down my face. I wanted out of this nightmare I'd gotten us into. I couldn't get enough air. I felt like I was breathing through a straw. "How are we . . . going to . . . get out of here?"

Henry grabbed my arms and held on tight. "Don't panic, Riley. We have to think!" He used his best adult voice.

Right. I had to get out of panic mode so I could think clearly. I wiped my eyes with my shirtsleeve and concentrated on slowing my breathing. *In and out, in and out.*

"Do you have cell phones?" Dr. Schwartz asked.

Henry snatched his phone and lit up the room. "Yes, we could call . . ." He stopped. "No signal."

"Freddy will come looking for us, won't he?" I grasped for the slightest shred of hope.

"Sure," Henry said. "He wouldn't just leave us."

"Who's Freddy?" asked Dr. Schwartz.

"He's our friend who drove us here. He's waiting outside. I hope he's still outside . . . unless . . ." I didn't want to say it out loud because it might come true. Marcus could find Freddy and tell him he was our teacher and he would take us back to the city and so Freddy could just leave.

"Maybe there's an area of the tunnel where we can get cell service," Henry said.

"Right, we have to keep trying. We have to think like Tesla," I said. "Dr. Schwartz, do you know where this tunnel leads?"

"To Tesla's tower, which no longer exists. He dug a large shaft, about a hundred and twenty feet deep." She spoke in a raspy whisper. "But it was filled in long ago."

Henry shined his phone around the cavernous chamber. "The tunnel leads this way. I'll go check it out. You stay with Dr. Schwartz."

"No! Please, I want to stay together." I turned to our teacher. "Can you walk?"

She nodded weakly. We helped her to her feet.

"What happened to you?" I asked.

"I came here to meet Marcus yesterday. He promised to give me the notebook, but it was a trap. He pushed me down the stairs. I fell and hit my head." She grimaced. "And I think my arm is broken."

"You've been down here all night?"

She nodded again.

I immediately felt sympathy pain in my scraped-up elbow. She didn't deserve this. She was just trying to give the world a gift and make sure it was delivered to everyone. That was what Tesla wanted. What Marcus wanted was to get us out of the picture he had drawn of himself as an engineering god.

We plodded along, taking tentative steps through the dark tunnel. I held on to the back of Henry's shirt with one hand and Dr. Schwartz's good arm with the other. The farther we walked, the older the tunnel appeared. The bricks and cement looked brittle and were crumbling apart. We stepped over metal pipes and wires.

If I could do it all over again, I would never have gotten us into this mess. "How could I be so stupid?" I mumbled to myself.

"It's not your fault, Riley. Marcus is a deranged monster." She strained to get the words out.

"Do you think he knows about the secret invention Tesla stored away?" I asked.

"No, there's no way he could know."

That didn't make a bit of difference now. We were going to be locked away in Tesla's tunnel forever. I shook that thought out of my head. Tesla said his visions were so clear, he could see them in front of him. I needed to envision a way out of here.

Henry's phone lit up the tunnel a few feet ahead of us.

"How much battery do you have left on your phone?" I asked.

"Twenty percent."

I checked my screen. "I have sixty."

"Okay, let's use mine until it dies."

"Can you please not use that word?" I said. My vision of our survival was still really blurry.

39

BELOW THE SURFACE

Henry stopped suddenly. "It's a dead end. There's just a bunch of dirt and rocks." He picked up a small rock and chucked it back down the tunnel.

"That's what I thought," said Dr. Schwartz. "The shaft Tesla built to the outside has been sealed off."

My chest tightened again. I pulled out my phone. My hand shook as I checked for cell reception—still no signal.

Dr. Schwartz stumbled. "I . . . I need to sit down. I'm really dizzy."

We helped her rest against a brick wall. I pulled out the water bottle that had been in my backpack for days and handed it to her.

"Thank you." She took a few sips.

"Dr. Schwartz. How far underground do you think we are?" Henry asked.

She looked at the ceiling as if she could see the outside. "I would guess the surface is about ten feet above the tunnel."

"Maybe we can dig our way out through the shaft and climb on top of the dirt. It might take a while, but we have nothing else to do," said Henry.

"It's possible," she said. "But the top may be sealed off some other way."

"It's worth finding out. We can at least get our cell phones closer to the surface while we still have battery left," he said.

"Yes, good idea! Let's try that!" I shouted.

"I saw some pipes and junk down the tunnel. I'll go see if I can find something to dig with."

"Okay, I'll stay with Dr. Schwartz."

Henry went off on his search and silence filled the tunnel like an underwater tank. All I could hear was myself breathing. *Don't panic. Don't panic.*

I paced back and forth, trying to think about life and not thinking about . . . the opposite of life. I hated that Marcus was going to get credit for being the inventor of wireless electricity. If we ever got out of this tunnel, I was going to prove he was a liar and a thief, but how? There were no cameras in this old building. Maybe footprints or DNA? He was really good at covering his tracks. "Maybe I could use my lie detector pen."

"Your what?" Dr. Schwartz asked.

"My lie detector pen. I forgot that you didn't get a chance to see my invention project. It's a pen that can detect when someone writes down a lie, but it doesn't matter anymore."

"That's amazing, Riley."

"Thanks. I wish you could see it."

She lowered her eyes. "I'm sorry. I'm a terrible teacher for getting a student involved in this."

"It's not your fault." I shook my head. "I should've asked for help. I thought I could handle it and get credit for being some super-investigator."

"Riley, I came here to look for Tesla's secret. The secret that you discovered. But I'm afraid it was just a silly treasure hunt."

I was too embarrassed to admit I came to search for the secret location too. If Dr. Schwartz couldn't find it, what chance did I have?

"To be honest, maybe I've become a little too obsessed with Tesla's discoveries," she confessed. "Part of me wanted to help secure his legacy. He died penniless while other people profited from his inventions."

"We can't let Marcus steal your work. We need you to finish your research."

Dr. Schwartz was silent and looked completely defeated. If I ever got out of this hole, I was going to make sure everyone knew the truth.

40

BREAKING TESLA'S CODE

I flashed my cell phone around the tunnel, checking for things that slithered or crawled. A pile of small bones lay in one corner—probably a rabbit or squirrel that had crawled down here years ago. I thought of my safe, cozy bed at home and wished I could transport myself under the covers. Why couldn't Dr. Schwartz have been working on teleportation?

She sat leaning against the wall holding her arm. She seemed to be dozing.

I wondered how many people built this tunnel. What tools could Tesla have had a hundred years ago? Brick by brick, building his invention. I ran my hand along the wall. Some of the bricks had numbers etched into them.

Was that important? Should I wake Dr. Schwartz? I blew on a brick to clear the dirt, sending a powdery dust into my lungs. I coughed and hacked and . . . woke Dr. Schwartz.

"Dr. Schwartz, some of these bricks have numbers written on them. Do you think there's a reason?"

"I'm not sure. What are the numbers?"

I called them out. "Three, five, seven, eleven, thirteen, seventeen, nineteen, twenty-three."

Dr. Schwartz's forehead creased. "They're prime numbers. It does seem like they're intentional, but I'm not sure why."

"Wasn't Tesla's favorite number three? Didn't he like things being divisible by three?" I asked.

"Yes, that's right."

I slid over to the number three brick and pushed it, knocked on it, and used my long legs to kick it. Nothing happened.

A shuffling sound came from down the tunnel. It was Henry, dragging something behind him.

"The good news is, I found some pipes to loosen the dirt. The bad news is, I lost a contact, so I only have one good eye." He studied our faces. We were too focused on the numbers to reply to him.

"What's going on?" he asked.

"There are numbers on the bricks, and they're all prime numbers. Look, Dr. Schwartz, there are more over here." I moved a little farther down the tunnel. "Twenty-seven, twenty-nine, thirty-one, thirty-seven, and then it starts over with two."

Henry covered his non-contact eye.

"Twenty-seven isn't a prime number," he said.

"You're right. But it's divisible by three. Twenty-seven divided by three is nine and nine divided by three equals three!"

"I'm way ahead of you, Riley." He tapped his head.

I pushed on the number twenty-seven brick and the cement around it crumbled. "It's loose around the edges." I pushed on one side and the other side poked out like a seesaw.

Henry grabbed the end with his fingertips. He wiggled it more and more and slowly pulled it out.

"What's in there?" asked Dr. Schwartz.

We shined the phone light through the hole where the brick used to be, but it was pitch-black inside. Henry put his hand in the hole, sliding it farther and farther inside. I stepped back, imagining what could be behind there—possibly skeletons or even worse . . . bugs.

"I can't feel anything. It's just a big hole." He pulled on the brick below the hole and it came right out. "Quick, pull on these bricks," he said.

We scrambled to pull the bricks down and they fell like dominoes. I hoped it was an escape route that Tesla built for emergencies—like the one we were in right now.

The bricks above the hole started to cave in.

"Step back!" Henry yelled.

Bricks crashed to the ground. Dust billowed up like smoke.

When the dust cleared, we saw a larger hole the size of a doorway. Henry shined the light inside. I stepped over the pile of bricks. Henry came in behind me.

"Wow! There's a whole little room back here." I coughed out some dust.

"It's like we stepped back in time," said Henry.

"What?! What's in there?" Dr. Schwartz asked.

"It's a small room full of old equipment: coils, meters, small machines made of metal." I spoke loudly so she could experience our discovery with us. "It's like a cement safe—a Nikola Tesla treasure room!" My excited voice echoed through the tunnel.

Dr. Schwartz managed to get up and peek inside the room. She didn't attempt to climb over the rubble. "Riley, I think this might be it. I think you found Tesla's hidden location!"

"We found it!" I called out to her. "But I'm still not sure what we found exactly."

To one side was a small table. It looked like it was carefully placed away from the tools and machinery. In the center of the table was a wooden box put on display like a royal crown.

"Henry, look at this." I waved him over.

I opened the box slowly, almost ceremoniously. Inside was a notebook, the same size as the first notebook. I picked it up and dusted off the cover.

"Dr. Schwartz, there's another notebook in here." I leaped over the bricks, back into the tunnel, and handed her the book.

She carefully scanned the pages, straining to focus. "Thank you, Riley. This is exactly what Tesla wanted us to find," she said with awe.

I soaked in the triumph. This new discovery made it feel like being trapped underground wasn't all that bad. But my enthusiasm was brief. Reality quickly returned.

"We have to get out of here so you can continue your research," I said.

"Um, and so we can live," Henry pointed out.

"Yes, right, of course!"

I helped Dr. Schwartz sit back down. She held the notebook to her chest and closed her eyes. She was in bad shape. Getting out of here would be up to one-eyed Henry and me.

41

THE ESCAPE PLAN

I stepped back inside Tesla's hidden room, amazed at all the objects he wanted to keep stored in a safe location. I secretly wondered how much it was worth and if it was an actual treasure—Tesla's treasure.

"There's a lot of history here," Henry said, shining his phone around. That was when I saw it. Something was different about the ceiling.

"Henry, shine your light up. I think there's a . . . a hole in the ceiling." A narrow opening, about the size of car tire, went straight up.

"What's it for? Where does it go?" His voice cracked at the sight of this new discovery.

I peeked around the corner. "Dr. Schwartz, there's a hole in the ceiling. Do you think it could go to the outside?"

"Yes! It's possible that Tesla wanted another way into his

secret room." She took a deep breath. "He knew his tower was being destroyed and all access to his tunnel might be cut off."

Henry strained to see with his one good eye. "I can't see all the way to the top, but if we can shove one of the pipes up into the hole, maybe we can break through to the outside." He grabbed the longest pipe and pushed it up. I helped him hold it steady, but the pipe didn't touch anything at the top.

"We must be short a few feet," I said.

"We can use the table to get closer. You have to do it, Riley. You're taller." Henry ran over and pulled the old, rickety table until it was directly under the hole in the ceiling.

I carefully stepped on top. My head was almost inside the dark hole.

Henry handed me the pipe. I pushed it up into the hole, inch by inch. When my hands reached the bottom of the pipe, I gave it one big shove upward.

"I hit something!" I cried. Dirt and debris rained down on my head. "It's a hard surface, but it's breaking apart. It sounds like tin."

I kept my eyes and mouth closed and hit the pipe against the ceiling over and over. I needed to conjure up all my strength and aggression. I thought of Dillon's smug smile when he showed me his invention. *Bang.* I thought of Marcus tricking me into believing his lies. *Bang.* My arms grew tired. I thought of Marcus hurting Dr. Schwartz. *BANG!*

Bigger chunks of debris came down. "Grab the pipe!" I yelled to Henry.

I knelt down onto the table, then jumped to the floor. I shook the dirt out of my hair and wiped my eyes with my shirt.

"Is everything okay in there?" Dr. Schwartz asked.

"Yes, Riley did it!" Henry cried. "She broke through to the outside." Daylight filled the hole all the way down into Tesla's secret room.

Henry hugged me. "Are you okay?"

"Yeah." I dusted myself off some more. We stared at the sky above.

"Let's see if we can get a signal." Henry looked at his phone. He shook his head. "My phone's dead."

One phone down. I handed him mine.

"There's still no service. We need to get the phone closer to the top of the hole, or even better, outside the hole. I would try to climb, but there's nothing to grab on to," he said.

"Maybe we can attach the cell phone to the pipe." I rifled through my backpack. The tape I used on my lie detector pen was still at the bottom. "Yes, hopefully this will hold."

Henry grabbed the end of the pole and I tried to attach the phone. "The pole is too dirty. The tape won't stick."

"I got this." Henry spat on the end of the pipe and wiped it with his T-shirt. "There."

"That'll work." I didn't even care how disgusting it was. These were desperate times. I placed my phone against the top end of the pipe and wrapped the tape around it.

"Here's the plan," I said, using my hands as arrows.

"I'll climb on the table again, then as soon as I press *send* on the phone, help me move the pipe up through the hole. OK?"

He nodded, then I typed a message: *Freddy, help! We're trapped in a tunnel under Wardenclyffe.*

I hit *send*.

"Now, go!"

Henry helped push the pipe up the hole until he couldn't reach any higher. With all my strength, I held the phone toward the daylight for what seemed like minutes.

"I can't . . . hold it." I pulled the pipe back down and jumped off the table, falling to the ground.

"It went through! Freddy will get the message." Henry smiled as he helped me stand.

"I hate to bring this up." *I really didn't want to bring this up.*

"What?"

"What if Marcus got to Freddy and broke his thumbs so he couldn't type or . . . he did something worse so Freddy could never, ever get the message?" I wasn't sure if my mind was just going into really dark places. We couldn't take that chance.

Henry looked down at the ground. "We can try a nine-one-one text. Come on. Let's do it again."

I typed the message, hit *send*, then quickly heaved the pole toward the ceiling. Once again, after a few seconds, I jumped off the table and fell to the hard floor.

"It worked!" Henry said. "Someone has to get our message now. We just have to wait."

"And if no one comes soon, we start digging." I pointed to the massive pile of dirt closing off Tesla's deep shaft.

"Dr. Schwartz, we got a message out," I said.

She forced a tiny smile. "Great job." She closed her eyes again. "I'm going to rest now. I'm not feeling well."

There was hope for our escape. I stared at the outside world above and took a deep breath. We weren't going to die in Tesla's tunnel.

42

A BUM RAP

Henry and I sat on the ground straining to hear any hint of human activity above. Dr. Schwartz dozed on and off. I told her we'd wake her if we heard anything. I touched her back a couple times to make sure she was still breathing.

I thought back to the events leading up to this moment, and I was filled with an overwhelming sense of guilt. It permeated every cell bumping around inside me. Henry would never want to be friends with me after this. He'd probably never even talk to me again.

"I'm so sorry, Henry. I'm sorry I dragged you into this. I'm sorry I made you follow me into this trap. It's all my fault. You tried to stop me." I covered my face. Tears turned my filthy hands muddy brown.

"Hey, it's okay. We're going to get out of here. Besides, it's been . . . an adventure," he said.

I let out a one-syllable laugh and wiped my nose on my sleeve. "Nice try. I should've listened to you. I wanted everyone to think I was important, but I'm just a joke. I'm sure everyone thinks so."

He didn't respond, which meant he probably agreed.

"Why do you think you have something to prove?" he asked.

That comment stung, but I wasn't sure why. "What do you mean?" I asked.

"It seems like you're always trying to justify being at Washington Prep. Like you don't belong there or something."

"I *don't* belong there," I shot back.

"Why? Did someone tell you that?"

I thought back but couldn't remember anything specific. So I thought back some more. Then way back. Someone at some point must have told me I didn't belong there, but who? Dillon? Valerie?

"It's just that I'm not the daughter of a senator or the granddaughter of a Supreme Court justice," I said. "I'm nobody."

"Your mom works for a senator. That's not nothing! My dad is always saying how he couldn't survive without your mom in his office. She keeps the place running."

"I guess so."

"Look at Abraham Lincoln. He grew up in a log cabin and . . . the Wright Brothers didn't even go to college and . . . Sonia Sotomayor grew up in the projects and became a Supreme Court justice. You can be anything you want." His voice trailed off.

"Wow. You really are a history buff," I said, very impressed with my friend.

"Thanks."

I sighed. "I just wish everyone at school felt that I was important."

"Are you kidding? You found Tesla's secret invention! That's the most important thing anyone has ever done at that school. Or maybe anywhere in electrical engineering history." He shook his head. "I would've given up on this a long time ago. I'm just a chicken."

"No, you're not. I think you're brave. You tackled Marcus!"

"It didn't do any good, but thanks." Henry hunched over, his arms on his knees.

"There's no way in a million years I could've done this without you, Henry."

He didn't answer. I wasn't sure what else to say. Henry was right about me. I did feel less important than everyone else at Washington Prep, but I had no hard evidence to back it up. It was like I had falsely accused myself of being an insignificant loser and convicted myself without a trial.

"Thanks for sticking by me," I said.

He shrugged. "You're welcome. I guess my lucky wristband is a bust. It doesn't work." Henry started to take it off.

"No! Keep it on . . . just in case."

I wanted to tell Henry I was the lucky one because I had him as a friend. I started to say it, but suddenly got shy, and then the moment passed. So I leaned against him and we waited.

43

YOU GO FIRST

Faint sounds drifted down into the hole. "Ri-ley. Hen-ry."
Was it Freddy?

We jumped up and screamed. "We're here! Down here!"

The sound of our names grew louder.

"Riley! Henry!" The voice was right above us.

"We're down here!" I yelled.

"Keep yelling!" the voice shouted back.

Dr. Schwartz woke up and joined in calling out for help.

Someone appeared above, the sun shining behind him. I
could make out a head with a ponytail. It *was* Freddy!

"Hey, down there!" he yelled. "I got your text."

"Freddy! You're safe!" I cried.

"Of course I am. I wish I could say the same for you. How
the dickens did you get down there?" he asked.

I let out an awkward laugh, an emotional mixture of relief

and sloppy happiness. "It's a long story, but listen, our teacher is hurt."

"And there's this crazy guy, Marcus. He may be after you!" Henry shouted.

"Tell him to call the police," Dr. Schwartz said.

"And call the cops!" I yelled.

Freddy looked around. "Is there another way in there?"

"Yes, there's a door inside the warehouse down on the lower level, but it might be locked. This could be our only way out," Henry said.

"I'll go check." Freddy ran off.

I kept my eyes glued on the opening, focusing on the light like a beacon of hope. We waited in silence for Freddy to return. I was a bundle of nervous tics—hand wringing, leg shaking, stomach growling. I was hungry on top of scared.

Dr. Schwartz cleared her dry throat. "Riley."

I rushed next to her and knelt down. Henry followed. "I won't be able to get up the hole if that's the only way out . . ."

I knew that already. "We'll call the fire department as soon as we can and tell them where to find you." I rushed out the words, trying to reassure her.

She nodded. "I need to ask you both a favor."

"Of course," I said.

"Once Marcus makes his speech, he'll get all the financial backing he needs." She spoke softly. "He could even sell the invention to the highest bidder."

I listened carefully to every word. "What can we do?"

"I need you to stall him until I can get there with the police," she said, quietly but firmly.

I looked at Henry. I wasn't going to make any other critical decisions without him. He nodded.

"Okay, we'll do it," I said.

A car engine hummed above us and a chain of dog leashes fell into the hole. Henry ran over and grabbed it.

Freddy appeared over the hole. "There's no way I can get through that door, so here's what we're going to do. There's a loop at the bottom of the rope of leashes. I need you to put one foot in the loop and hold on tight while I pull you up, one at a time."

Henry and I looked at each other.

"You go first," we said together.

"No, really." I pleaded. "I want to watch you go up." I got us into this mess—it was only fair that I got him out first.

"Okay." He climbed onto the table and placed one foot into the loop. He locked his legs together and held on tight. "I'm ready!" he called up to Freddy.

Freddy disappeared, then Henry slowly moved up like a fish on a line. Thank goodness our librarian/chauffeur was built like a professional wrestler.

I glanced at Dr. Schwartz. She looked so frail. "Don't worry," I told her. "We'll find a way to prove Marcus is guilty of everything—destroying your classroom and your lab, sending death threats, locking us in here, and stealing Tesla's notebook."

She smiled weakly. "I hope you're right."

Freddy—and Henry's head—blocked the light coming into the tunnel.

"Your turn, Riley! Grab on!" Freddy lowered the rope of dog leashes.

I stepped into the loop and hugged the rope as tightly as I could. They pulled me up slowly. I spun around and hit the side of the hole, but I made it to the top, where Henry and Freddy pulled me over the ledge. I filled my lungs with all the air I could handle. *Too much. Too much.* I coughed and wheezed and hacked out some dust.

I looked over the hole. "Dr. Schwartz?"

"I'll be okay, Riley. Please, go! You have to stop him!"

The three of us jumped into Freddy's Town Car and I called nine-one-one. I told the dispatch person everything that had happened—a mad scientist named Dr. Marcus Smith trapped us under Wardenclyffe and our teacher was still down there. The story was so wild, I sounded like a prank caller. I wasn't sure she believed me.

I knew Freddy believed me because he kept shaking his head. And he was gripping the wheel so hard, his knuckles turned white. After I hung up, I told Freddy about Tesla's missing notebooks. He had earned the right to know. He had saved us from certain death.

"I'll get you there as quick as New York City traffic will allow," he said. "Sit tight."

I hated leaving Dr. Schwartz all by herself, but the police and fire rescue would be more help than we would.

Henry and I looked like a couple of stray dogs riding in the back of the pet taxi. We were dirty from head to toe. I pulled my hair back with a rubber band, then wiped my face with my shirt. That would have to do. I just hoped we weren't too late.

44

THE GHOST OF TESLA

Bumper-to-bumper traffic surrounded the New Yorker Hotel. We could see the building but we were boxed in by cars, trucks, and construction. Freddy, Henry, and I had worked out a plan in the car to keep Marcus from making his speech. It wasn't foolproof, but it was all we had.

My legs were antsy, and I couldn't wait any longer. "Come on, Henry, let's make a run for it!" I opened the door in the middle of the street and jumped out.

Freddy leaned out the window. "I'll be right behind you as soon as I park this tank!"

He laid on the horn.

Henry and I dodged a delivery truck, weaved around a taxi, then stopped just before we got to the front door of the New Yorker Hotel. I brushed off my shirt, and we casually waltzed through the revolving door. Luckily for us, the lobby was busy with guests because we stuck out like we had just escaped from a dingy dungeon. Which we had.

A sign in the lobby directed engineers to the second floor. I pulled Henry toward the escalator and we stepped on. I felt completely exposed. We needed a disguise, but there was no time for that.

About halfway up, I spotted adults mingling about in front of a set of double doors. A banner above the doors welcomed members of the Institute of Electrical and Electronics Engineers.

"Look. There," I said, quickly followed by, "Wait. No!" I ducked down and yanked Henry with me. We knelt on an escalator step.

"What's wrong? I can't see." Henry squinted.

"It's Marcus."

"Should we run back down?" he asked.

"No. Follow me."

We stayed crouched on the step and rode the escalator to the top, then jumped off and ran into a large ballroom. Rows of chairs faced a giant video screen that was surrounded by curtains. "Come on!" We ran behind the curtains into a backstage area.

"Now what?" Henry asked. "We were supposed to find a fire alarm and pull it, remember? That was the plan."

"I know, but I didn't see one and I wasn't about to wander around in the open. We'll have to improvise." We sat in panicked thought, which was not at all effective. I remembered the look on Dr. Schwartz's face when she said, "You have to stop him."

The buzz in the ballroom grew louder. The seats were filling up.

We had to find something to use as a distraction. I looked around backstage. There was a podium, sound equipment, and extra chairs. Then a wild idea hit me. It was absolutely bonkers, but it was all we had to stall Marcus until Dr. Schwartz could get here.

"Henry, you have to be the ghost of Nikola Tesla," I whispered.

"You want me to be *what*?"

I scavenged around the equipment. A cordless microphone sat on top of a rolling podium. A soundboard was tucked on the shelf underneath. With any luck, the speakers would be out in the ballroom.

I scrolled through my phone, searching the internet for recordings of Tesla. There was only one recording of him ever made.

"Here's the plan. We're going to play a recording of the real Nikola Tesla, then you'll be his ghost."

I waited for him to protest, but he didn't.

"You won't have to be in front of anyone. You can stay here behind the screen." I held out my phone and the microphone.

He looked at the ground, then nodded at me. "Okay, I got this."

I flipped the switch on the soundboard. The speakers came to life with a loud crackling noise. Henry hit *play* on my phone and the voice of Nikola Tesla echoed throughout the ballroom.

"Electric power is everywhere present in unlimited quantities. It can drive the world's machinery without the use of coal, oil, gas, or any other fuel. This new power, for the driving of the world's machinery, is going to be derived from the energy which separates negative earth—the cosmic energy."

I jabbed my finger at Henry. "Say something," I mouthed.

"This is the ghost of Nikola Tesla." Henry faked a deep, sophisticated voice. "The genius inventor who brought you the Tesla coil and alternating current technology . . . and the neon sign. It's a little hard on the eyes, but very energy efficient."

Laughter broke out in the ballroom. Apparently, people thought it was part of the presentation. I peeked around the curtain, checking for Marcus. There was no sign of him . . . yet. I waved my hand at Henry, urging him to keep going.

"It is so nice to see so many engineers here today. I want to tell you about my invention of wireless electricity. . . ."

"Tell them Marcus is a fraud," I whispered.

"Yes, you see, I came back from the dead to tell you that this man, Dr. Marcus Smith, is a fraud!" The laughter stopped. "He wants to take credit for *my* invention! Smith is a thief and a liar!"

"He's coming!" I yelled. Marcus ran toward the video screen.

I grabbed Henry's hand. He dropped the microphone, but it was too late.

45

SLEIGHT OF HAND

Marcus stared at us as though we were a couple of ghosts. Henry and I were supposed to be dead—or at least on our way to being dead.

"What? How?" His face turned red, and he gritted his teeth. "You were supposed to die in that tunnel. Now I'll have to come up with another way to silence you two." He grabbed my arm. Henry grabbed my other arm. I was in the middle of a tug of war.

"Hey! Let her go!" shouted Freddy as he ran up behind Marcus. He bent over, resting his hands on his knees, breathing hard.

"Or what?" Marcus shot back.

"Or the coppers are gonna put bracelets on you and cart you off to the big house," Freddy said like an old-timey detective hot on the case.

"Get out of my way," Marcus said with disgust. He tried pushing Freddy aside, but he was too big. Freddy pushed back, grabbed Marcus by the suit jacket, and pulled it down his arms so that it trapped them behind his back. Then Freddy kicked Marcus to the ground and kneeled on top of him.

"Wow, Freddy. You should add ninja warrior to your business card!" said Henry.

The sound of banging chairs and handheld radios reverberated throughout the ballroom.

"Police! Put your hands up!"

Freddy raised his hands in the air and slowly stood up.

"Kids, come over here!" shouted another police officer.

Marcus stood up and smiled broadly at the police officer. "Thank goodness you're here. This man attacked me!"

I balled up my fists except for one finger that I pointed directly at Marcus. "He's a liar. This man threatened our teacher and a senator, and he tried to bury us alive."

Henry moved over to Freddy. "Freddy rescued us . . . twice."

"Put your hands up!" The police ordered Marcus.

"I did nothing wrong," he argued. "This is all a big misunderstanding."

Henry pressed *play* on the recording app on my phone. "You were supposed to die in that tunnel," said Marcus's recorded voice.

The police cuffed him in front of a large group of engineers who were witness to an unexpected detective show. The scene was nothing like you see in the movies or read in Raymond

Chandler books. This was real and I felt lucky to be alive.

I watched Marcus get carted away in handcuffs. I finally saw him for the criminal he really was. I found it hard to believe Marcus's despicable deeds were all because he wanted to be known as a famous inventor. *What some people will do to feel important*, I thought to myself. Then I thought about myself. Right then, I decided I was never going to worry about that again, because I already was a very important person.

I hugged Henry. "Your phone recording is even better than my lie detector pen!" He smiled.

"Your teacher is waiting upstairs," said a police officer. "She refuses to go to the hospital until she sees that you two are safe."

We ran up the escalator and into the lobby just before the paramedics were about to wheel Dr. Schwartz outside and into the ambulance.

"Dr. Schwartz!" I yelled.

"Thank goodness you're okay. You were both so brave," she said in a whisper. She looked at Freddy. "And thank you for rescuing us."

"You're welcome," he said like a humble giant. "I'm glad everyone is safe."

"I'm sorry we didn't get the notebook back, Dr. Schwartz. But maybe we can still get it now that Marcus has been arrested."

Freddy cleared his throat. "Do you mean this book?" He held up Tesla's notebook.

I gasped. "But . . . how?"

Freddy handed the book to Dr. Schwartz.

She held the notebook tightly to her chest.

A paramedic stepped in front of us. "Okay, time to go to the hospital. You can visit her when she's in recovery."

She waved with her good hand. I waved back. She was going to be okay.

Freddy leaned over.

"I promise not to tell anyone about the notebook," he said. "I'm no snitch."

"How did you get it?" I asked again, completely amazed.

"Let's just say I've watched enough sleuth TV to know how to pilfer a pocket."

"You picked Marcus's pocket?" Henry asked, checking his own pockets.

We all laughed even though it wasn't that funny. We were just tired.

Another police officer approached. "I'll need statements from all of you before you can leave, and we'll need to contact your parents."

Henry and I exchanged glances.

We collapsed on a sofa in the hotel lobby, each taking turns yawning in a wave of exhaustion.

"Hey, Riley, do you think you could put in a good word for me with your teacher?" Freddy asked. "Maybe I could help her with her invention. You know, that would be something important."

"Absolutely." I smiled. "As soon as we get home."

I was so ready to go home, and I was ready to tell Mom everything. I wanted her to know about what happened on my *real* spring break. The story of Riley Green was one of utmost importance.

46

THE INVENTION CONVENTION

On the day of the schoolwide Invention Convention, I realized something about my lie detector pen—I had never tested it on myself. I wasn't sure it would work on the person asking the questions, and I wasn't about to try now. My hands were so fidgety, my handwriting would be worse than Henry's.

The gym was a frenzy of activity with students frantically setting up their invention projects to impress the judges. I double-checked the connections on my prototype. The USB wires were fastened to the pen and securely plugged into the laptop. The wires made writing a little awkward, which might skew my results, but I had several samples to back up my claims. The judges would have to look at my drawing to imagine what my actual lie detector pen would look like. Hopefully, that would be enough to prove I was the true inventor of the lie detector pen.

I moved over to Henry's table. "Have you seen Dr. Schwartz?"

"Not yet," he said with a mouthful of gumball.

Henry and I had become minor celebrities since spring break. News about our adventure had spread faster than gossip, except it was actually true. Students didn't know all the details, but they knew Henry and I had helped find the person who had wrecked Dr. Schwartz's room. They also knew we had been trapped in Tesla's tunnel and saved Dr. Schwartz's life. So far, we'd managed to keep the part about Tesla's notebook a secret.

Charlotte trotted over to us. "Hey, y'all. I'm so nervous, and I'm not even in the competition." She giggled.

"I'm not nervous at all," said Henry. I gave him a look because I knew better.

A momentary hush came over room. I looked over the crowd. Dr. Schwartz had arrived with a bandage on her head and her arm in a cast. Walking beside her was her father, the Professor.

"Dr. Schwartz and the Professor are here!" I told Henry.

"What! I'm not ready!"

Dr. Schwartz walked straight to our displays. "Hi, kids. You remember my father." She gestured toward the Professor.

"Good morning." I fixed my posture and clasped my hands behind my back.

Henry swallowed his giant wad of gum. "Hello, Professor."

"I asked the Professor to be a judge for the schoolwide competition. We needed someone who was a little more impartial than I might be." Dr. Schwartz winked at us.

The Professor examined my invention. He had another badge around his neck, except this one said INVENTION CONVENTION JUDGE.

He muttered the occasional, "Uh-huh, hmmm," then said, "Don't you need a handwriting sample of the culprit before giving them the lie detector test?"

"Yes, sir. Excellent question." I pointed to my display. "I created this document designed to collect information such as name, address, and other questions we know to be true. For example, one question is, 'Describe the clothes you are wearing.' In doing so, the pen collects valuable data about the formation of each letter. The last question is an open-ended question about the alleged crime, such as, 'Where were you on the night of April second?'"

"Interesting. Let's give this invention a whirl, shall we?" The Professor grabbed my pen off the table and prepared to write.

I placed a copy of my data collection form on the table and crossed my fingers. Doing that was not scientific at all, but it couldn't hurt.

While the Professor completed the top portion of the form, I thought of a question that would catch him in a lie. It had to be a good one. *Okay, got it.*

When he finished, I whispered in his ear, "Where is Tesla's secret notebook?" I knew he couldn't tell the truth. He smirked as if to say, "That's pretty clever, Riley."

He began to write, and I stared at my computer screen.

Please work, please work. Dr. Schwartz looked as nervous as I was, waiting for the results. The seconds crawled by like a slug inching forward, and my stomach felt like I had just eaten one.

After the Professor completed two sentences, the computer blinked "FALSE" on the screen.

"It worked!" I accidentally said out loud. I wasn't supposed to be so surprised.

"Well, I'll be," said the Professor. "This is terrific. You need to get a patent on this idea, so no despicable thieves steal it."

That was the best compliment I could've gotten, but I had one question. "How do I get a patent?" I asked Dr. Schwartz.

"You can apply for one with the United States Patent Office. That would protect it from being developed by someone else. I can help you if you'd like."

"That would be great," I said.

"Well, I have to keep going. Good luck, kids." Dr. Schwartz strolled to the next invention.

Charlotte quickly slid up next to the Professor and whispered something in his ear. Her whispers were usually loud enough to hear, but not this one.

Charlotte led him away. She glanced back and waved for me to follow them. *What was she up to?*

We walked straight to Dillon's display. I stood behind the Professor and peeked over his shoulder. I was almost too nervous to watch.

Dillon wore a suit and tie and quickly introduced himself. "Hello. I'm Mr. Dillon Walker, son of Senator Walker, and inventor and proprietor of the Lie Buster Pen 2000."

2000? Really? What does that even mean?

"Hello, Dillon. Can you demonstrate your invention?" the Professor asked.

"Of course. My assistant, Michael, will show you how it works. First, I'll ask him to write his name, and then he'll write a made-up name."

The Professor interrupted Dillon's sales pitch. "Actually, I think you should demonstrate it yourself."

Dillon hesitated, then gripped the pen. "Sure, no problem. Ask me any question."

"First, I'd like to know if the pen has recorded your natural handwriting?" said the Professor.

"Yes, sir. My pen knows my handwriting and is as accurate as fingerprints," Dillon answered.

"Okay, then, Mr. Dillon Walker, how did you come up with the idea for a lie detector pen?" Dillon thought for a moment, then wrote something about wanting to catch liars. The light on the end of his pen blinked *red, red, red.*

"According to your display, the red light indicates a lie," said the Professor.

"There must be a glitch in the pen." He shook it like a maraca.

"So, you're saying your invention doesn't work?"

"No, no, it works," Dillon said, still managing to hold on to a smile.

"How about I tell you what to write," said the Professor.

"Um, I don't think it works that way." Dillon's smile was fading fast.

"Let's give it a try, shall we? I want you to write, "'The idea was Riley's, and I copied it.'"

Dillon froze.

"Go ahead now," said the Professor, pointing to the piece of paper.

Dillon scowled, then wrote it, and the pen blinked green.

"How about that? It *does* work," said the Professor.

This time, Dillon was the one who looked as though he'd gotten punched in the stomach. He was busted by his own lie detector pen. *Sweet revenge.*

"Your admission of guilt disqualifies you from the competition. I need to confiscate your project and report your cheating to the principal," said the Professor.

Dillon's face had panic written all over it. "You can't do that. My father . . ."

The Professor crossed his arms and raised his bushy eyebrows. "I tell you what. I'll talk to the principal about you serving detention at the Smithsonian and helping me catalog artifacts . . . for a month!"

Dillon's nose scrunched up as if the room was filled with the smell of cabbage, but he finally relented. The Professor took his pen and presentation.

I wasn't sure how to feel. Dillon looked so pathetic, standing there empty-handed, but then he glared at me with a red face. "What are you looking at, String Bean?"

I turned to leave when a completely uncharacteristic comment came to me. I spun around. "You know, Dillon, I'm not sad that you stole my idea. I'm sad that you didn't have any ideas of your own." I dashed out of there before he could say anything.

Okay, so I paraphrased Tesla, but I couldn't let that one go to waste.

I caught up with Charlotte. "Thanks for busting Dillon." I nudged her.

"You're welcome. Come on, let's go get some gumballs from Henry," she said.

We crossed the room, and I found my math teacher studying my invention. I darted over like I'd been there the entire time.

"Hi, Riley. Is this your invention?" she asked.

"Yes, ma'am."

"This is a significant idea. Do you have any writing samples?" she asked.

"Absolutely." I showed her my notebook and pointed out the change in the shape of the letters and weight of the pen marks.

"Great job!" She wrote on her judging sheet and strolled to the next invention. I tried to peek at her clipboard, but I couldn't see. Maybe next year I'd invent a pen that memorizes writing, so the words can be reproduced, kind of like an eavesdropping pen. *Brilliant.*

I glanced around the room looking for my two best friends. The electricity in the air was contagious and it wasn't the electric current kind—it was the excitement kind.

I found Henry and Charlotte shooting gumballs at each other. I laughed out loud. Henry's invention wasn't going to win any awards, but it sure was a big hit.

"Hey, Riley! Catch!" Henry said, shooting one at me.

There was one thing I didn't need my lie detector to tell me. If my body were a giant mood sensor, it would be glowing a bright blue.

Let the future tell the truth, and evaluate each one according to his work and accomplishments. The present is theirs; the future, for which I really worked, is mine.

—Nikola Tesla

HISTORICAL FACTS INCLUDED
IN THIS STORY

Nikola Tesla died in 1943 at age 86 in his room at the New Yorker Hotel. After receiving news of his death, his nephew Sava Kosanovic rushed to his hotel room but discovered that his uncle's body had already been removed. He believed someone had gone through his things and had taken technical papers as well as a black notebook.

Some of the missing papers were believed to include several hundred pages of notes, many of them marked "Government." Still in the midst of World War II, the Office of Alien Property hurriedly confiscated two truckloads of Tesla's documents from various locations so they wouldn't fall into enemy hands.

Tesla was one of the most prolific inventors in modern history. He was born in Smiljan, Croatia, on July 10, 1856, and exhibited an early interest in technology. He studied electrical engineering and physics in France in the 1870s. It was there that he conceived the concept of the alternating current (AC) power distribution system.

He then moved to the United States to work for the famous inventor Thomas Alva Edison. Ultimately, Tesla disagreed with Edison on the method for distributing electricity and left the company so he could further develop his concepts of alternating current motors and power distribution systems.

It is not an exaggeration to say Tesla's alternating current inventions ushered in the modern age of electricity and are arguably the foundation of the modern technical world we live in today. He was awarded around 300 patents. In the 1890s, one particular technology that was the focus of his research involved the wireless transmission of power. In 1899, Tesla traveled to Colorado Springs to perform wireless experiments. He created structures in a barn that included large coils and a mast that held a metal ball high in the air. He was able to create very high voltages in his structures that resulted in spectacular